TORN APART

PETER CORRIS is known as the 'godfather' of Australian crime fiction through his Cliff Hardy detective stories. He has written in many other areas, including a co-authored autobiography of the late Professor Fred Hollows, a history of boxing in Australia, spy novels, historical novels and a collection of short stories about golf (see petercorris.net). In 2009, Peter Corris was awarded the Ned Kelly Award for Best Fiction by the Crime Writers Association of Australia. He is married to writer Jean Bedford and lives in Sydney. They have three daughters.

PETER CORRIS

TORN APART

ALLEN&UNWIN

Many thanks for all kinds of help, to Jean Bedford, Miriam Corris, Ruth Corris, Tom Kelly and Jo Jarrah, and to an officer of the NSW Police media liaison unit.

All characters and events in this book are fictitious. Any resemblance to actual people and circumstances is coincidental.

First published by Allen & Unwin in 2010
Copyright text © Peter Corris 2010

Allen & Unwin
83 Alexander Street
Crows Nest NSW 2065
Australia
Phone: (61 2) 8425 0100
Fax: (61 2) 9906 2218
Email: info@allenandunwin.com
Web: www.allenandunwin.com

Cataloguing-in-Publication details are available from
National Library of Australia
www.librariesaustralia.nla.gov

Internal text design by Emily O'Neill
Set in 12/17 Adobe Caslon by Midland Typesetters Pty Ltd, Australia
Printed and bound in Australia by Griffin Press

10 9 8 7 6 5 4 3 2 1

For Miriam, Philip and Axel

Irish poets, learn your trade,
Sing whatever is well made

W B Yeats

part one

1

The surgeon who took out the bullet that had nearly killed me told me that I needed to lead a quieter life. Interesting choice of words. After the death of Lily Truscott, my partner of several years, a heart attack and bypass surgery and a near fatal bullet wound, I agreed that I needed something. But what? A new profession? I'd been a private detective for most of my adult life, and although that was closed to me after losing my licence for various infringements, the work, for better or worse, had become part of me and I couldn't imagine doing anything different. A new location? I'd been in Glebe so long that it felt like my habitat, my natural environment.

I'd inherited a lot of money from Lily. Guilt came with it because I hadn't put the same faith in the relationship. I helped my daughter Megan out, fixed up the house, paid some overdue debts and lived on the capital. I didn't really need—that word again—to work, but I didn't know how else to occupy myself. I didn't fish or play golf and you can only read so many books, see so many films, listen to so much music.

The solution was no solution at all, just an interim measure—a holiday. The idea gave me something to think about. The problem with inactivity is not just the inactivity itself but its accompaniment—having nothing to think about. I was used to having my head full of assumptions, misgivings, theories to do with whatever I was working on. I'd mentally trawl through cases for similarities and differences and process lists of names to help or obstruct. I missed all that.

Reading brochures and the travel sections of newspapers and magazines, recalling books set in exotic places, checking the posters in travel agency windows wasn't a substitute for my kind of investigation, but it occupied some brain cells. Talking to people was better, tapping their memories good and bad.

'I wouldn't advise Iran or Iraq,' Ian Sangster, my friend and GP, said. 'In fact I wouldn't leave Australia with your recent medical history. You seem to be totally recovered, very fit in fact, given what you've been through. But you never know, and if something went wrong your medicos'd need your bloody medical records.'

'Thanks a lot, Ian. You reckon I should think about somewhere close and calming, like Hobart.'

We were sitting at a table outside the Toxteth Hotel having a late morning drink. Ian was smoking and already well into his first of the two packets he'd smoked every day for thirty years.

'You might think about it. You could look for the graves of your convict ancestors.'

'Did that once, or someone did it for me. A couple ended up in Camperdown cemetery, so they're now under the sod where dogs shit and people do tai chi.'

'Just a suggestion.' He butted his cigarette and stood. 'And another thing, don't go off on your own. Find someone to go with you.'

That was a problem. I had other friends and I had a daughter, but no one I could think of who'd want to up stakes and take off as a travelling companion to someone who'd been knocked about as much as me. Even though I could pay.

I remembered what my mother—a hard-drinking, heavy-smoking, piano-thumping descendant of Irish gypsies—used to say when my father, a dour, sober man, bemoaned a difficult circumstance: 'Never you mind, boyo. Something'll turn up.' For her, it mostly did, and right then it did for me when I met my cousin, Patrick.

He'd tracked me down somehow on the internet and when he rang me I was struck by the similarity in our voices. 'I'm your cousin, Cliff,' he said. 'My grandad was your grandma's brother.'

'That right?' I said. 'She had a sister or two, I know, but I never heard of a brother.'

'Yeah, well I gather Grandad was a bit of a black sheep.'

'The way I heard it they were all black sheep. Gypsies.'

'They weren't gypsies.' He sounded annoyed. 'They were Irish Travellers.'

That was interesting and news to me. I'd only met my grandmother a few times when I was a kid. She was old, very dark, very wrinkled. I remembered that she shook her head and told my mother that I'd have an interesting life but wouldn't make any money. I guess she was right on both scores. I hadn't *made* the money. My mother always referred to herself as a gypsy and played up to it with scarves and rings and bracelets.

'Sorry to be so abrupt,' he said. 'Look, why don't we get together and have a drink and a yarn? I can fill you in a bit about the Travellers if you're interested. To tell you the truth, you're the only relative I've got left in the world.'

Why not? I thought. I asked a few questions and learned that his surname was Malloy. That figured. It was my grandmother's name and my mother's, her being illegitimate. He told me his age. He was a year younger than me. We agreed to meet the following day in the late afternoon at Kelly's Hotel in King Street, Newtown.

'I'll shout you a Guinness,' he said in exactly the kind of mock Irish accent I used to put on to the annoyance of my ex-wife, Cyn.

With time on my hands and not wanting to appear too ignorant, I did some quick web research on the Irish Travellers.

Not Romany at all, it appeared, but indigenous Irish, the descendants of people who took to the roads centuries ago, no one quite knows when or why. Nomadic like the gypsies, followers of appropriate trades—like dog and horse breeding and selling, holding market stalls, dealers in second-hand goods. They apparently had their own language and customs and there was a strong musical tradition among them. That fitted Granny Malloy all right, who could sing like a bird in old age and play the fiddle. My mother had the same talents and I remembered her using odd words that she said she picked up from her mother. I'd assumed this was Romany talk, but maybe not.

Kelly's Hotel has an unusual history. It's on the site of the only known failure of a McDonald's franchise in Sydney. There's too much good food at reasonable prices along King Street for the cheap burger joint to flourish. The area has become so gentrified that a booth there recorded the highest Green vote in the state. Greenies don't go to Macca's.

The place has a cosy feel, with a ramp sloping gently up to the bar and tables and seats on either side. It handles the Irish theme well: there's the imitation snug and the barrels, but it's mostly a matter of tasteful photographs of Irish scenes—not a shillelagh in sight. It does light lunches and dinners and has the inevitable trivia competition one night a week. Lily and I went in for it once with Frank Parker, my ex-cop mate, and his wife Hilde, and got cleaned up by a table of youngsters who knew all about TV stars and bands later than Dire Straits.

When I arrived there were only two tables occupied—one up near the bar and one near the front. I told the barmaid I was waiting for someone and took a seat in the middle of the space, off to one side. It's an old habit of mine to try to get a good look at someone I haven't met before he, or she, sees me. You can learn a bit from body language and mannerisms. I also try to be early for the same reason and because it can give you an insight into the habit of the other person: early might mean anxious, on time might mean obsessive; late might mean slack. Or not.

A lot of people passed in the street and a few came in and settled down to their drinks. I looked at my watch and about two minutes after the appointed time a man walked in with the air of someone unfamiliar with the place and hoping to be met. Two minutes late didn't mean anything in my analysis. But it wasn't the timing or his manner that caught my attention. This man was tall, well built, with dark hair going grey. He looked fit. He also had a beaked nose that had been broken at least once and white scar tissue from boxing threaded through his heavy eyebrows. In other words, he was a mirror image of me.

2

I got up and we shook hands.

'He laughed. 'You're surprised.'

'You aren't?'

'I saw a photo of you in a newspaper. I was surprised then all right.'

He insisted on shouting. We took our pints of Guinness into a corner and touched glasses.

'So,' I said, 'second cousins. I didn't know I had any. The Malloys and the Hardys weren't exactly great breeders.'

'Likewise. My mother was an only child and I'm the same.'

I told him I had a sister who had two children I'd scarcely ever seen because they lived in New Zealand.

'A nephew and a niece, eh? I suppose they're some relation to me, but I'm buggered if I know what you'd call it.'

The similarity in our voices and manner seemed to have

the same effect on us, making both of us quiet, unsure of what to say. He wore slacks and a blazer with a business shirt and no tie. I was in cords, a football shirt and denim jacket.

'Well, Patrick,' I said, 'there's one difference at least—you dress up a bit.'

He laughed and that broke the ice. We finished the drinks and I got up to get a round. 'I might . . .'

'Make it just a middy,' he said, patting his stomach. 'Got to watch the flab.'

That was exactly what I was going to propose and for the same reason. I watched while the drinks were being poured. Patrick seemed at ease, very still, perhaps unusually so. The beer loosened us up and we chatted. He told me that his grandfather had been adamant that he came from a line of Travellers, not gypsies, and that recently he'd taken an interest in the subject and had looked it up in books and on the web. Malloy was a Travellers' name, he said, but so were lots of others.

I drank and nodded, mildly interested, but with a question looming larger in my mind. *Who is this guy and what is he?*

He broke off. 'I'm boring you.'

'Not a bit.' I touched the scar tissue above my eyebrows. 'Weird that we've both got this. You boxed?'

'In the army and very, very briefly as a pro. Saw the error of my ways and quit. You?'

'Amateur only. Before the army and after.'

'Jesus,' he said. 'Talk about parallel lives.'

A few stories had appeared in the papers about me in recent years, all negative and to do with the loss of my PEA licence. I'd withheld evidence, been accused of conspiracy to pervert the course of justice, and been given a lifetime ban. So he knew about me. Time to get on a level footing.

'What's your game, Patrick?'

'I've done a few things in my time, Cliff. Did a law degree after the army and worked for a couple of unions. Then I went into buying and renovating old pubs around the place. Here, there and everywhere. Made a good quid at that. Now I've got some investments and a share in a small security firm. That's mostly hands-off but occasionally I have to step in and do a bit. What're you up to these days?'

'Nothing much. I've got enough money to skate along.'

He nodded. 'Tell you what, my firm's handling the security for the Moody/Sullivan fight on Wednesday week. It's sold out, they tell me, but I've got some tickets. How'd you like to come along as my guest? Be ringside.'

The Moody he was talking about was Mick 'Mighty' Moody, the current Australian middleweight champion and the son of Jacko Moody, who'd held the title twenty years before. I'd had some dealings with Jacko and other La Perouse Aborigines back then, and I'd followed Mick's career in the papers. There was talk of a non-title fight with Anthony Mundine but his management was bringing him along cautiously. Time was on his side. Mick was only twenty and these days, with better diet, training and fewer, shorter bouts, boxers can last into their thirties. I was keen to see the fight and said so.

'Great,' Patrick said. 'I'll send a car to pick you up. Parking's a bastard at the pavilion.'

'I can get a cab.'

'You'd be going as my guest. It's my pleasure.'

I thanked him and gave him the address. We shook hands again and went our separate ways. That put my holiday on hold for a while, but I hadn't come up with a workable plan anyway. I spent my time in the ways I'd begun, reluctantly, to get used to—going to the gym in Leichhardt, swimming at Victoria Park, hanging out with Frank Parker and Hilde, dropping in on my daughter and her partner Hank Bachelor. I was reading through a batch of Penguin Hemingway novels I'd picked up second-hand in Gleebooks and playing pool with Daphne Rowley in the Toxteth Hotel. And religiously taking my meds.

I was collected by a guy driving a white Commodore and wearing a uniform with patches that said 'Pavee Security'. The word rang a bell but I couldn't place it. His name tag read Kevin Barclay and I was glad that he didn't say he was there to help. Too many Kevins these days did. He didn't talk much on the drive. The fight was a big event with extensive media interest and Patrick was right—parking was a problem all around the Hordern Pavilion and the driver had to keep his mind on the job to avoid angry motorists and work his way to where only the privileged few could go. He got me close to an entrance and handed me a ticket.

'Enjoy the fight, Mr Hardy.'

'Thanks. Will you be inside, Kev?'

'Some of the time.'

'Expect any trouble?'

'Nah, well, I could let you in on a secret.'

'Yeah?'

'Better not. I'm saying Moody by a knockout in the fifth.'

I puzzled over his remark as I presented the ticket and was escorted down a couple of levels and along an aisle to a seat in the second row with a square-on view of the ring. There's something unique about a boxing program that infects the audience before it starts. You know a fight can be a long, testing affair or over in a matter of seconds. No other sporting contest is like that. The place was packed and noisy and that atmosphere of tense uncertainty drove other thoughts from my mind. The front row is too close. It spoils the perspective, and further back you miss some of the nuances. Row two is perfect.

The preliminaries weren't much. A couple of footballers were making their debuts, one as a heavy and the other as a light-heavy. They won against opponents even less skilled than themselves. Seemed to me they should have stuck to football. The six-rounder before the main event was better. A fast, rangy Lebanese lightweight named Ali Ali boxed the ears off a stocky opponent for four rounds before unwisely deciding he could mix it in the fifth. A solid left rip to his unguarded mid-section put him down and after taking an eight count he walked into a straight right that ended his night.

Patrick arrived just as the referee reached ten and the crowd, as crowds will, roared its approval of the KO.

'Evening, Cliff. How's it going?'

'Pretty good. Ali should've stayed on his bike.'

'You're right.' Patrick, wearing a dark suit over a white T-shirt, looked around. 'Bloody good house. We'll make a quid.'

'You're the promoter?'

'One of them. I've got a piece, as the Yanks say.'

'Expecting any trouble security-wise?'

'Never can tell. Boxing 'n' booze are a potent combination. Fancy a drink?'

The ringside area was catered for by a squad of waiters wearing a smarter version of the Pavee uniform, and the rest of the auditorium was serviced by a bar at the back. I don't like the idea of drinking while men are sweating and hurting each other and I refused. Patrick nodded, ordered mineral water from the waiter, and settled back as Sullivan and his party came down the aisle to the ring.

As always, the half-naked women who hold up boards for the round numbers waited to greet the fighters. It's a fairly recent addition to the circus, geared to television, and the

14

traditionalists don't like it. But if they'd had the idea in the old days and could've got away with it, they'd have done it.

There was nothing flash about Moody. He entered the ring only a few minutes after Sullivan and no martial music played. Sullivan was the number one contender for Moody's title, a crown he'd held himself in the past. He was a veteran with an impressive record but a couple of losses that had stalled his career. He was stocky, pale, heavily tattooed. Moody was tall and lean, teak-coloured and severe-looking in a grey hooded top and dark shorts. The announcer gave their names the usual pizzazz; they were both under the middleweight limit so the title was definitely on the line. The referee gave them their instructions and the bell sounded.

From almost the first few minutes it was clear that Moody had the edge. Not that Sullivan was unskilled; he knew how to defend and attack, but, compared to the younger man, he was slow. Not by much, but in boxing split seconds are crucial. His speed advantage by hand and foot enabled Moody to land his punches more cleanly and more often and to avoid most of Sullivan's responses. The crowd urged Sullivan on, but by the seventh round he was tiring and frustrated. He tried a bullocking rush; Moody sidestepped and caught him flush on the ear with a stiff left. Sullivan floundered and Moody, his moment having arrived, drove him to the ropes and landed heavily on his head and body. The referee stopped the fight.

'He's good,' Patrick said as we moved to leave. 'Picks his spots.'

'Have you got a piece of him, too?'

'Hey, come on, what d'you take me for?'

'Sorry,' I said. 'I have a love/hate relationship with the game.'

'I know what you mean. No, I steer clear of the managerial side. Strictly an administrator.'

We went out to where the white Commodore was parked and Patrick said he'd given Kevin the night off and would drive me home. I felt obliged to invite him in for a drink and we talked amicably. He saw *For Whom the Bell Tolls* lying open and said he was a great admirer of Hemingway. I asked him about the name of his security outfit and he said Pavee was the name the Irish Travellers gave themselves. I'd read that but forgotten.

'You're really into all that, aren't you?'

'I am. Dunno quite why. It's an interest.'

We parted as something like friends.

The next time I saw him was a week or so later at the Victoria Park pool. He swam more laps than me with a slow, powerful stroke better than my surfer's choppy action. We had a coffee afterwards and he drew a line down the centre of his chest with an index finger.

'You're in the zipper club?'

'Yep. A while ago now. I had a heart attack in America. Lousy medical system if you're poor, but probably the best in the world if you're not.'

'That's what killed my dad. Quite young, poor bugger.'

'Mine too. You look fit, Pat. You *are* fit, but you must be about the same age as me and with the family connection and all it wouldn't be a bad idea for you to have a check-up. I didn't see it coming.'

'I'll do that.'

He rang me a few days later to say that he'd had the tests and they'd found a blockage.

'Not as serious as yours must've been,' he said. 'I have to have this thing called a stent. No big deal. But I'm glad you alerted me. Look, they want me to go into hospital for a day or two. D'you mind if I put you in as next of kin? Just a formality.'

'Sure. I never asked—no wife or kids?'

'Divorced years ago. No kids that I know of.'

'I'll visit you.'

I did. He had a private room in Strathfield Private Hospital. The nurse who escorted me to the room looked at me with wide, startled eyes.

'I know,' I said, 'we're cousins.'

'You look like twins.'

He came through the minor procedure with no trouble but was annoyed to learn that he'd be on a couple of medications for the rest of his life.

'You get used to it,' I said. 'And the daytime ones you can wash down with a glass of wine.'

He grinned. 'Is that what you do?'

'Between us, yes, sometimes.'

'Well, thanks for coming and not bringing grapes.'

I handed over the Hemingway novel, which I'd finished, shook his hand and left. At the nurses' station I heard a man asking where Patrick was. He was pale and ginger-haired and he did a double-take when he saw me.

'I'm Patrick's cousin,' I said. 'He's doing fine.'

'Glad to hear it. God, I thought you were him making a break.' He laughed and stuck out his hand. 'Martin Milton-Smith, a colleague of Patrick's. Good to meet you.'

We shook. 'Cliff Hardy.'

I thought he reacted to the name but I couldn't be sure. He smoothed down a silk tie that nicely matched his suit, and went down the corridor in the direction the nurse had given him.

'Does Mr Malloy get many visitors?' I asked the nurse.

'So far only two—you and him.'

A few days later Patrick appeared at my door in the late afternoon. He had two cans of draught Guinness in a paper bag and the Hemingway book in his hand. He came in and we went out to the back area I'd bricked amateurishly years ago. I could have had it relaid when the other work on the house was done but there was something about it, lumpy and with grass growing through the cracks, I liked. We lifted the tabs on the cans and poured the brew carefully into glasses.

'Cheers,' he said. 'Looks to me as if you're doing bugger-all.'

I drank. 'That's about it, Pat.'

'Me too, more or less. I've got an idea. I'm thinking of going to Ireland to look up the Malloy Travellers. Why don't you come with me?'

3

We flew Qantas business class to London. Patrick had grown a beard and had his hair cut short so that more grey showed. With that and his smarter clothes, we didn't look as much like the Bobbsey Twins as before. We hung around London for a few days. We'd both been there before and we went off separately renewing old memories. In fact we didn't spend much time together. He was a late sleeper and I'm an early riser. I used buses to get around and he used the tube. We had dinner together only one night, but here again our preferences were the same—Indian in Old Brompton Road, with hot curries, plenty of naan and cold beer.

The dollar was fairly strong against the pound but neither of us was economising. We'd arrived in May and the weather was warm, much warmer than I'd known it to be there before.

'They'll be having to take their socks off and just get around in their sandals if this keeps up,' Patrick said.

'When were you here last, Pat?' I asked.

'About twenty years ago.'

'Doing what?'

'Why?'

'Just curious.'

He ate another mouthful before answering with another question. 'How about you?'

I shrugged. 'Twelve years back. Missing persons case.'

'You find him?'

'Her. No.'

'I was dumb,' he said. 'I missed the army when I left. The marriage had finished and I was pretty pissed off. Would you believe I signed up in Sydney with a mercenary outfit?'

'That *was* dumb.'

'Yeah. A bunch of us came over here. Did some training in Yorkshire and the word was we were going to Angola. I'd wised up a bit by then. It was a gimcrack mob, half pisspots and half psychopaths. I went to Australia House, dug out some newspapers and read up on the civil war in Angola. There was no way I was going to get into that.'

'So what did you do?'

He laughed and took a big swig of lager. 'I fuckin' deserted, mate.'

We took the train to Liverpool and caught the ferry to Ireland. It was a rough, four-hour crossing and we spent most of the time in the bar.

We were drinking Irish whiskey, getting in the mood. After a particularly rough spell I said, 'We could have flown and avoided this.'

'I wanted to make the crossing the way our people coming out to Australia would have done back then. No aeroplanes.'

No Jamesons or hot snacks either, I thought, *but let him have his fun.*

Patrick read his way through a batch of newspapers he'd picked up and kept me abreast of things in the UK. I liked the response the new Lord Mayor of London made to the standard tabloid interview question 'Have you ever had sex with a man?' Boris Johnson replied, 'Not yet.' Great answer.

I was reading Tim Jeal's biography of Henry Morton Stanley, the man who 'found' David Livingstone. It was interesting, particularly the stuff about the way people in those times could completely reinvent themselves. Like Stanley, like Daisy Bates, like 'Breaker' Morant. Stanley, the American, wasn't Stanley and wasn't an American. And he probably didn't say, 'Dr Livingstone, I presume.' I suppose people can still myth-make, but it must be harder these days. I looked up from the book from time to time to study our fellow passengers. They mostly seemed comfortable, even affluent—had to be to pay the bar prices. The English and the Irish seemed to be on good terms, which would have surprised and angered Granny Malloy.

We'd booked a hotel and arranged to hire a car. We were

sharing expenses, but Patrick had his top-of-the-range notebook computer and was in charge of such things and doing it well. We'd agreed that I'd do the driving and he'd do the navigating. I was surprised that he accepted the more passive role and asked him about it.

'I had a pile-up a while ago, Cliff. People got hurt. I don't fancy driving these days.'

'You drove me home from the fight.'

'I was being nice.'

Dublin was cold, misty and wet but the car, a big Mitsubishi SUV, was delivered to the hotel door. We loaded our light luggage into the back and there looked to be room for three or four times as much.

'Why the monster?' I said.

'The Travellers are impressed by big vehicles. We don't want to look like pikers, and we might have to go off-road here and there.'

That made sense and I enjoyed the feel of the powerful engine and the comfort of the car—air con, CD player, hands-free telephone set-up, GPS facility. Patrick had equipped himself with a map, plotted our route, and only resorted to the GPS for confirmation.

We took our time driving across to the west. The weather was typically Irish—damp and changeable. We experienced different kinds of weather within a period of a few hours. It was nothing like driving in country Australia, no long straight lines to the horizon. Off the major roads, the narrow bitumen and clay stretches bent and curved and rose and fell and crossed creeks that bubbled and would never run dry. We went south to County Clare and visited Tipperary like the tourists we were. We stopped here and there to take in the scenery, have a drink and some food. I experimented with the new phone camera Megan had given me as a birthday present but had trouble sorting out its functions. As befitted men for whom the cardiac alarm had sounded, we went for longish walks around the stopping places, climbing some pretty steep hills and not rewarding ourselves too handsomely in the pubs and eating and sleeping well. The Irish have the bed 'n' breakfast thing down to a fine art.

It was evening when we reached Galway. Good time to arrive, with mist shrouding the bay and giving the town itself a nineteenth-century feel. Like mine, Patrick's mental image of Ireland had been formed by reading about the slaughters under Cromwell and William of Orange, the famine and the troubles; by films and photographs and music—the Clancy Brothers, the Chieftains, Sinéad O'Connor. The strange thing was that the picture in the imagination and the reality were pretty close. The green of the fields and hills was intense, almost too much for Australian eyes used to more muted colours. And the sea was grey-blue and I imagined I could hear Ewan MacColl's voice as I looked at it.

We walked down to the water's edge, crunching across the pebbles, and Patrick unzipped his fly.

'I swore I'd do this,' he said. 'It's out of respect.' He let a strong stream of urine arc into the lapping water.

I picked up a pebble, worn smooth and white by wind and waves, and put it in my pocket. 'I'll settle for this as my symbol,' I said.

Over a pint in O'Leary's in Eyre Street, Patrick filled me in on our destination. He'd spoken vaguely about Galway and I'd been happy to go along with that. Who, visiting the Emerald Isle, doesn't want to go to Galway? My mother had vamped the chords of the Bing Crosby song on the piano and warbled the words with an accent thicker than any Irish stew.

'We're heading for Ballintrath—inland a bit, back towards Dublin.'

'Okay, why?'

'They hold a big fair there—not as big as the one in October but pretty big and a lot of horse trading goes on. I mean, literally. The Travellers are great horse breeders and traders and the Malloys have a reputation in that game.'

'So we just bowl up, find some Malloys and say, "How're you going? We're Malloys from Australia"?'

'Something like that. Why not?'

Strange to say, that's pretty much how it worked out. Ballintrath was a well-preserved medieval town geared up for tourists and visitors. This fair was a scaled down version of the one in October apparently, but it was pretty busy with the usual market stalls, events in pubs and other venues around the town and the equestrian side of things taking place on the Fair Green—a big expanse that was slowly turning to mud under the pressure of feet and hooves.

The events centred on competitions for the best in a number of categories, most of which didn't mean anything to a city man like me. Best foal I understood.

Patrick hunted out an organiser and asked if there were any people by the name of Malloy present.

'To be sure. Why're you askin'?'

Patrick explained.

'Travellers, is it? Well, they keep pretty much to themselves. They have a camp outside the town somewhere. But Old Paddy Malloy you'll find over yonder at the farrier judgin'. He's a judge and plays the fiddle as the shoein' goes on.'

We wandered over to where three farriers were engaged in a competition to see who could shoe the horses the quickest and the best. The crowd was four or five deep around the roped off area where the contestants, but not the spectators, were protected from the drizzle by a sail. It was only that Patrick and I were taller than most of them that we were able to see much at all. The fiddle cut through the muttering and murmuring of the spectators with clear crisp notes. Through the nodding heads I glimpsed a white-bearded man fiddling energetically while watching the competition. The farriers seemed not to hurry but they were getting the job done. One finished clearly ahead of the other two. The music stopped when the last hoof went down and the crowd applauded enthusiastically.

'Pretty good,' Patrick said to a man standing in front of him. 'Who'll win?'

'Why, Sean Malloy,' the man said. 'Always does. He's not the fastest but he's the best.'

The winner was declared, the dark nuggetty type who'd finished second. It didn't seem to worry anyone that the judge and the winner were related. The crowd drifted off to other attractions or perhaps to get under cover, although the drizzle didn't seem to have bothered them, as the horses were led away. With our coat collars turned well up, we approached the fiddler and Patrick introduced himself and supplied some details about our origins.

'You're never Mick Malloy's grandson—him as went to Australia?'

'I am,' Patrick said—the idiom was catching.

The dark eyes, young-looking in an old face, turned to me. 'And you. Christ, you're like peas in a pod but for the beard.'

'Grandson of Aideen Malloy,' I said.

'Aideen. There was a one, so I've been told. Well, well, all the way from Australia. That's famous, that is. You have to come to the camp and meet us all.'

We ferried a couple of car-loads of Malloys and others to the camp a few miles to the east of the town. The track was muddy and Patrick's opting for a 4WD proved to be the right decision. The Travellers clan had campervans and trailers rather than anything resembling gypsy caravans, but they'd decked them out and painted them in ways no ordinary tourers ever would, with banners and slogans proclaiming their identity.

Sean Malloy, the winning farrier, had a grip of iron and bore a few boxing scars. So we talked fighting and over cups of strong tea and door-stop sandwiches we roughly established the relationship of us both to the thirty or so people in the camp. Then it was off to a nearby tavern for the adults where a *céilidh* was scheduled, with a few of the Malloys slated to sing and play.

For me, the evening was a bit of a blur, not so much from the drink, but from fatigue and the noise and the smoke. The tavern was an old cottage, gutted so that there was a long open space with a bar at one end and chairs and tables scattered about. The night was cold and the windows were closed so that a thick fug of tobacco smoke, sweat and alcohol fumes quickly built up.

We weren't allowed to pay for anything, which kept me going slow with the grog. The music was heady, emotional, traditional stuff that touched off tears and joy in everyone present, especially when old Paddy played the fiddle to a tenor lament from his nephew Sean. But that mood was quickly replaced by jigs and reels in which Patrick and I joined with nothing like the lack of inhibition of the locals. I opted out and went to find a corner to gather my breath and my wits.

'Hello, Aussie,' a woman sitting nearby said. 'Conked out have you, mate?'

The accent was genuine Australian.

'I'm buggered,' I said. 'A bit old for this.'

She pointed with a long, thin arm at where the dancers were. 'Your mate's doing okay.'

'He's a bit younger. I'm Cliff. You are?'

'Angela Warburton, from Coogee.'

We shook hands. 'Know it well.'

She was fortyish, dark, with a mass of red-brown hair, green eyes and a strong face. I was a bit drunk and I took out my mobile phone, still experimenting, and snapped a picture of her. Just for fun I pointed the lens here and there and took some more pictures.

'They'll be lousy in this light,' she said, 'and you should've asked permission. I'm a photo-journalist and I'm trying to do a spread on the Travellers. They're sensitive about photos. I have to go carefully.'

'You're right. Bad manners. We should be going if I can drag Pat away.'

She handed me a card. 'Look me up if you come back through London. You can tell me how Coogee is these days. I've been away for seven years.'

'I can tell you a decent house costs most of a million bucks.'

She shrugged. 'Would you believe it's getting to be the same over here.'

I put the card in my pocket and located Patrick sitting down after a dance and deep in conversation with old Paddy. When I said we should be off, Paddy wouldn't hear of it. We ended up staying another hour in the tavern and bedding down in sleeping bags in one of the vans.

Patrick spent four days with the Travellers. After being politely interested for the first day, I got bored with the talk of horses and which Patrick was related to which Michael. I caught a bus into Galway, booked into a hotel and spent the time walking around the town and its outskirts, fossicking in the second-hand bookshops and visiting various pubs. There were black and Asian faces in the streets and I got the impression that the immigrants were opening businesses and that Galway was in for some big changes.

Despite the Irish heritage, I didn't feel a particular connection to the place, unlike Patrick. My paternal grandmother was French, and I wondered whether I'd feel more at home in Paris where I'd never been. Perhaps next time.

I finished the Stanley biography and traded it in for a biography of Rimbaud. My taste was for the stories of people who led creative and active lives, and Rimbaud fitted the bill.

On a grey morning, Patrick collected me in the SUV and we stopped at the first bank for him to cash some traveller's cheques.

'I wouldn't say they bled me,' he said, 'but they didn't refuse my generosity. I said your goodbyes.'

'Thanks, Pat. It was interesting, but a bit rural for me. You going in for horses when we get home?'

'I don't know what the fuck I'm going to do. But it was grand.'

'It was,' I said.

We both laughed as we sprinted to get out of the rain.

4

We took our time on the return trip, followed the coast north and crossed into Northern Ireland. Patrick said he wanted to get to the place in Belfast where Van Morrison got his start and that was okay by me. We'd bought CDs of *Moondance* and *Tupelo Honey* in Galway and played them all the way. We never found the Maritime Hotel, but we heard some great music in other places.

My image of Belfast came pretty much from the film *The Boxer*, which proved to be fairly accurate. The city had a grim look and feel, although the military presence that had aroused such hatred was much reduced.

'One of the blokes in that bullshit mercenary outfit I told you about was ex-British Army,' Patrick said. 'He reckoned the Brits kept the trouble here on the boil as a cheap way of training troops.'

'Wouldn't surprise me,' I said. 'Nothing more useless than an idle soldier.'

'That's true. That's very true.'

We stayed in Belfast for longer than I'd have wanted and then Patrick insisted on going back to Dublin.

'The Malloys told me there's a terrific bookshop with everything ever written about the Travellers. I have to go there, Cliff. D'you mind?'

What could I say? I put it partly down to him apparently being reluctant to leave Ireland. We stayed at the same hotel as before and I used the gym and a heated indoor pool to try to stay in shape, given the beer and the amount of food you inevitably eat on a holiday. Patrick said he'd found the bookshop specialising in works about the Travellers.

'They let me sit and read there,' he said. 'It's marvellous.'

'You'll have to lash out and buy something eventually.'

'I will. When I'm ready.'

'When d'you want to head back, Pat?'

'Never, mate. No, don't look like that. I'm joking. Pretty soon, pretty soon.'

That sounded a bit strange, as if he had a definite schedule to meet that I wasn't aware of. That made me curious. Also, I was getting bored and that's probably another reason why I decided to follow Patrick one day when he set off after telling me he was skipping our usual breakfast at the hotel.

I'd spent years watching for changes of behaviour in people and then watching them as they moved about. It was my stock in trade and I couldn't resist the urge to give it a go in Dublin town.

'I'm off to the bookshop,' he said. 'Buying something today, and we should talk about a flight. Okay?'

I skipped breakfast, too. I picked him up in the street, staying on the other side and keeping close to other walkers. I told myself I was seeing if I still had the old skills.

Patrick didn't go anywhere near the stretch that featured the city's many and varied bookshops. Dublin had an efficient light rail system that I'd used a few times. Patrick bought his ticket at a stop where there was a fair-sized crowd waiting. I hung around on the fringes and bought my ticket when the double car swung into view. Patrick got into the first carriage and I got into the second.

It was a tricky situation; if he was the only one to get off at his stop and turned back he'd spot me. I'd have to go on to the next stop and hope to catch him when I doubled back. But I was in luck; he got off in the midst of a bunch of passengers and all of them moved forward so that I could hang back again. It was raining, a plus—hurrying people and umbrellas are always a help.

Patrick turned into an arcade and tracked the shop numbers as he consulted a slip of paper. He opened a door and went in. I waited before I moved past. The place was a veterinary clinic. I kept going and took shelter from the rain in a pub.

I'd enjoyed the exercise. It looked as if Patrick was getting serious about horses.

Patrick was quiet that night, almost morose. Just to make conversation I asked him if he had any ideas about what business to get into when he got home. He sparked up a bit.

'Have you got a proposition?'

'Me? No.'

He nodded. 'I have a thought or two.'

We flew from Dublin to London and caught a connecting flight home. During the stopover Patrick shaved his beard off because it was itching. So we looked very alike again. We were in the bar at Heathrow when Patrick grinned over his third whiskey.

'Want to have some fun, Cliff?'

'I might.'

'Let's swap passports and tickets. See if we can get away with it.'

I'd had a couple myself and was tempted, just for the hell of it. He took out the documents and waved them.

'Show them their security's not worth a pinch of shit.'

I looked around and took in the warnings about leaving baggage unattended, the urgings to report anything suspicious and the security men standing about, bristling with firearms and communication equipment.

'It's not worth the risk,' I said. 'Level of paranoia's too high.'

He sighed and put the papers away. 'Guess you're right. It's a terrible time to be getting old in, to be sure.'

On the flight Patrick sent and received text messages and I asked him how his business was doing.

'Running like clockwork. I'm selling it, didn't I say?'

'No. And then . . .?'

He shrugged. 'Something'll turn up.'

My grandmother's grand-nephew repeating her words.

He said he'd given up the flat he'd been renting and would be looking for something to buy. I offered to let him stay at my place while he looked and he accepted.

Patrick moved into the spare room with little more than the light luggage he'd taken on the trip, apart from a fiddle he bought in Ireland and the duty-free Jamesons, of course. He said the rest of his possessions were in storage and that he knew what sort of flat he wanted and in what area, so the business wouldn't take long. I was glad of the company and, as we were both more or less in limbo, I thought us bouncing ideas about our different futures off each other might be useful. Patrick was determined to learn to play the fiddle, but I wasn't up for that.

I lent him the Falcon to get around in because most of the places I wanted to go—the gym in Leichhardt, Megan's place in Newtown, the bookshops and eateries in Glebe and Newtown—I could reach on foot or by bus. After the damp of Ireland it was good to be back in a spell of crisp, dry Sydney winter days—while they lasted. I paid some bills, caught up on some films, visited Frank and Hilde and took my meds. I found life a bit flat, politics boring, and time hanging heavy, but Patrick was amusing and he never scraped away at his fiddle beyond 9 pm.

I got back from a gym session in the mid-morning, opened the door and knew something was wrong. A smell, a sound, or just a feeling?

'Pat?'

There was no answer. Nothing was out of place in the living room or the kitchen. It was moderately untidy like always, but the back door was wide open and the cordite stink was unmistakable. I pushed open the door to the back bathroom and the smell and the sight rocked me back and had me grabbing for the doorjamb for support. Patrick Malloy didn't look like me anymore. He didn't look like anyone. Most of his head had been blown away; an arm was hanging by a thread and his chest was a mass of raw meat and splintered bone. He'd been torn apart. The plastic curtain was shredded, and the walls in the shower recess were like a mad abstract painting in red and grey.

5

I'd shot a man dead in the house many years ago and had been shot there myself quite recently, but those events were nothing like this. The police determined that Patrick had been killed by three blasts of heavy load from an automatic shotgun. The first would have killed him; the others were about something else altogether.

Chief Inspector Ian Welsh of the City Major Crimes Unit who headed the investigation called me into the Surry Hills Centre for an interview two days after the SOC people had done their work. A folding table had been set up in his office and on it were the things Patrick had in the house at the time of his death, including the fiddle. I'd given permission to the police to take the stuff away on the condition that I watched them pack it up and had an itemised list signed by the detective in charge.

Welsh, thin, fiftyish, tired-looking, had Patrick's passport open when I entered the room and he stared at the photo-graph, at me, and back at the photograph, but made no comment.

The killing had shocked and saddened me and I hadn't slept well for the last few nights. Patrick was one of those people who filled a room, filled a house, but wasn't a nuisance. He had a knack of knowing when I might want coffee and when I might want quiet; when I wanted music and when I didn't. Seeing his fiddle lying on the table like an exhibit broke me up a bit. I sat in the chair Welsh indicated, reached out and picked up the bow.

Welsh put down the passport and examined a document in front of him. 'Thanks for coming in, Mr Hardy. I've read your statement. You've been very cooperative.'

I fiddled with the bow, nodded, said nothing.

'You've no idea why . . . your cousin—'

'Second cousin,' I said, 'and friend.'

'—why this could have happened to him?'

I put the bow back on the table. 'None.'

'You travelled overseas, you put him up in your house, lent him your car, but you don't seem to know anything about him.'

'I know the things he told me and they seemed enough at the time. Our family relationship, a bit about his past and the business he'd been in. We had interests in common—books, music, boxing . . .'

'You never felt the need to know more? After all, you used

to be a private enquiry agent. I'd have thought curiosity was your middle name.'

'I suppose I would've found out more as we went along.'

'He sought you out, you said.'

'Yes, this family thing about the Irish Travellers, we . . .'

'Yes. Did it ever occur to you that he needed you for protection?'

Given what had happened, it was a reasonable question, but from his suddenly alert manner there appeared to be more to it. He picked up the passport and flicked through it as he waited for my answer.

'No,' I said.

'Did he do business of any sort while you were overseas?'

That was a new tack and on the money, now that I knew what Patrick's visit to the vet in Dublin had been about. You go to vets for steroids the way you go to Mexico for Nembutal. But I didn't feel like enlightening Welsh.

'Not that I know of.'

He closed the passport and put it back on his desk. It was the only item separated from the other things—the fiddle, clothes, books, keys, shoes, a wallet, some photographs, a shell from the beach at Galway Bay.

'Thank you, Mr Hardy. That'll be all. I'll get an officer to see you out.'

'Hang on. What was that all about? Those questions?'

He touched a button on his desk. 'Don't concern yourself. We'll keep you informed of any developments that involve you.'

'You think I'm just going to walk away?'

'You'd better, Mr Hardy. You're not a private detective anymore.'

So that was just about that as far as the cops were concerned, but I wasn't having any of it. I'd liked Patrick, was grateful to him for suggesting the trip and had felt comfortable in his company. I knew that I'd miss him and that made it personal.

Welsh phoned, said the body could be released, and did I want to make funeral arrangements.

'Did you contact that company he owned?'

'Part-owned. Of course.'

'Anyone there know anything about his personal affairs— lawyer, will, that sort of thing?'

'I'm only responding because you seem to be the person closest to him. The answer is no. He scarcely involved himself in the business at all. Usually just when something big was on.'

'They must know something.'

'I've got no more to say. Are you going to make arrangements or not?'

Of course I agreed. I put a notice in the paper and arranged for the simplest disposal Rookwood could provide. Patrick hadn't gone to church during our trip and I'd never seen any signs of religious faith from him.

Megan phoned when she read the news in the paper and so did Frank and Hilde. They knew that I'd been fond of Patrick and his funeral wouldn't be easy for me. They each said they'd attend.

'Thanks,' I said to Frank. 'I wouldn't like to be the only one there for the poor bugger. Frank . . .'

'I know what you're going to say. Could I use my contacts to monitor the police investigation for you?'

'What's your answer?'

'I doubt it'd do much good. People in the service know about our connection. Anyone with information's liable to clam up if I get nosy.'

'Not everyone.'

I heard his groan. 'Okay, I'll do what I can but don't push too hard, Cliff. How's your heart?'

'Beating strongly, unlike Pat's.'

'I'll see you at the cemetery. There's something you should consider, if you haven't already.'

'What's that?'

'It could've been meant for you.'

I had thought about it, briefly. I had enemies who bore grudges—plenty of enemies, plenty of grudges. I avoided certain individuals and places, watched my back. There were people who'd want to get even, but I couldn't think of anyone who'd want it badly enough to go to this extreme.

Rookwood can be pretty bleak at the best of times, but the good weather spell had gone and the day of the funeral was overcast and damp. Not cold, though. It reminded me of Ireland, and it was a sure bet there were plenty of the Irish planted there. My father was there somewhere in a grave my sister, who was fonder of him than me, had looked after until she moved to New Zealand. Must've been pretty overgrown by now.

The ceremony in the crematorium chapel was the usual soulless affair and the mourners numbered seven—a man named Dan Munro representing Pavee Security, Frank and Hilde, Megan and her partner Hank Bachelor, me, and a police officer named Stanton who introduced himself and retreated into the background. Standard police procedure— they turn up at funerals of people whose deaths are being investigated just to see if anyone of interest is present.

After the business was over, Frank went into a huddle with Stanton, who smoked a cigarette and looked uncomfortable.

Frank spoke to me later when we'd adjourned to a back room in Kelly's.

'Pretty close-mouthed,' he said, 'but I gather they're not making much progress. One thing—they're suspicious of him, but they're not sure why. What d'you think, Cliff?'

I waited while Declan Donovan, a Glebe folk singer I knew, tuned his banjo. I'd asked him to play a few songs to give the event a bit of cheer and he agreed to do it for all the Guinness he could drink. That'd run up a fair tab along with what the rest of us drank, but it was the least I could do for Patrick.

With Declan strumming quietly, I said, 'I'm just going on instinct, but I don't see him as a big-time criminal player. A cutter of corners maybe, but . . .'

'Secretive?'

'We're all secretive. You are, I am. We have to be.'

'Philosophy, now?'

I shrugged as Declan launched into 'The Wild Colonial Boy', playing the upbeat Irish version followed by the slow Australian lament. He did 'Lily of the West' and 'Roddy McCaulay' to wring tears from your eyes, and a long rendition of 'With My Swag on My Shoulder' that had us all shouting the chorus line '. . . like a true-born Irishman'. Dan Munro left after one drink, but a few other people, like my doctor Ian Sangster, and Daphne Rowley, turned up.

It was a good bash—Pat would've loved it.

When I said we were all secretive I meant it. Circumstances sometimes demanded it. For example, if Welsh had been more forthcoming, less dismissive, I might have told him that Patrick had posted a package to my address from London. I'd done the same, just some books I'd bought in Charing Cross Road. I didn't know what Patrick had sent. He'd mentioned buying some DVDs and CDs of some fiddle players and I'd just assumed it was something like that. Maybe not.

You have to allow up to ten days for a package to arrive from the UK, so I had a few days to wait. Another thing was Patrick's mobile phone. He'd borrowed a jacket of mine and hung it back up in the cupboard under the stairs where it belonged. When I went to wear it, I found the phone in the pocket. Didn't tell Welsh for the same reason. The police hadn't asked about it—slack of them. That gave me two things to look into. I thought I might be able to get something out of the Pavee Security driver, Kevin, remembering his enigmatic remark. I wasn't expecting to nail the killer, just to give the investigators some lines to follow. Or so I told myself.

I like to think I'm not a complete Luddite, however the intricacies of Patrick's mobile were well beyond me, but they were Hank Bachelor's bread and butter. I took the phone to his Newtown office, the one I'd vacated in his favour after losing my licence. Hank, an American who found it impossible to live in a country run by the Bush administration, had been what he called my apprentice. He'd acquired his own PEA licence and was doing well.

'Thought you'd turn up,' Hank said when I arrived.

Hank is a caffeine addict and I'd brought along two King Street long blacks to smooth my path.

'I'm your de facto father-in-law. Why shouldn't I drop in?'

Hank took a long, appreciative sip of the coffee. 'Couldn't leave it alone, could you?'

'I'm planning to assist the cops.' I put the mobile on the desk.

Hank moved it around with a pencil. 'Top of the range. Patrick's?'

'Yep.'

'Unknown to the police?'

I nodded and drank some coffee. 'I'm wondering what might be stored in there—numbers, photos, passwords, codes . . .'

That's the thing about digital technology freaks; whereas most of us yearn for the simple and straightforward, they revel in the cryptic and the unrevealed.

'I'd like you to put it through your mental sieve, mate,' I said. 'Make it give up all its secrets.'

6

I phoned Pavee Security and asked to speak to Kevin Barclay. When I was asked who I was I told the truth. When asked in what connection I wished to speak to Mr Barclay, I said he'd driven me to the boxing some weeks back and that I wanted to continue the interesting conversation I'd had with him then. That seemed to be satisfactory, and I was given a mobile number. I rang it.

'This is Kev.'

'Mr Barclay. My name's Hardy. You drove me to the Moody fight.'

'I remember. The spitting image of poor Pat.'

'That's right. I wonder if we could meet? I'd like to talk to you.'

'What about?'

'Face to face. I'd make it worth your while—say a hundred bucks for twenty minutes.'

'That's a good rate. You know the Square Leg pub in Redfern?'

'Yes. When?'

'How about twelve thirty? I've got an hour break and you can buy me lunch. Do I get two hundred for forty minutes?'

I laughed. 'We'll see.'

It felt like being back in the saddle except that there would be no client paying the expenses. Didn't matter; the feeling was payment enough.

The Square Leg is old style in architecture, fittings and décor. It's not as if it's seen better days, it's almost as if the downbeat appearance is carefully maintained. The bar took me back to the pubs I used to drink in as a young soldier and a failing student. The advertisements are for brands of beer no longer brewed and the walls display pictures of horses and sportsmen long forgotten. The food on offer is basic— meat and fish, chips and salad—and they're still described as counter lunches. I got a middy of light and settled down at a laminex-topped table to wait for Kev.

I was early; he was on time. He came bustling in, a big, overweight man who looked as if he might have been a footballer in his youth before beer and sitting behind the wheel blew him up. Drivers typically have waiting time to fill in, and a lot of them cure the boredom with calories.

He plonked himself down at the table. 'Gidday, Hardy. I'll

have a schooner of old and a steak and chips—well done.'

I got his beer and ordered the meals, same for me.

'Good health.' He raised the glass and drank almost half. 'Not in uniform, Kev?'

'Nah, part-time job with Pavee. Doing courier work today. Pretty good fight, wasn't it? Pat's last fight.' He lifted the glass in a token toast. 'Pity that. Good bloke, Pat.'

Our number was shouted from the servery—none of your vibrating pagers at the Square Leg—and I collected the plates, the plastic cutlery, the tomato sauce sachets and paper napkins on a tray. Barclay finished his schooner as I put the tray down and I went to the bar for refills.

He was chomping enthusiastically when I got back and I let him get a few mouthfuls and swigs down before putting my questions.

'I want to ask you about a remark you made when you drove me to the fight.'

Still chewing, he nodded.

'What did you have in mind when you said you'd let me into a secret? It was after I'd asked if you expected any trouble.'

He was working on another mouthful and he held up a hand to signal a wait until he had chewed and swallowed.

'Why?' he said.

'I liked Pat and I don't like what happened to him. I want someone to pay.'

'Fair enough. I was a bit pissed and should've kept my trap

shut, but what I was going to say was that sometimes—only sometimes, mind you—Pat arranged for some trouble to happen at a place we were doing the security for. Nothing too serious, but just so word got around that we were useful and up to the job. You understand?'

He sawed off another piece of steak, pressing down hard, and speared some chips. I'd given up on the tough meat and was investigating the rather limp salad. I'd told Frank Parker I thought Patrick might cut corners without knowing why I thought so, but here was confirmation.

'Interesting,' I said. 'How many people know about that?'

'Just a few.'

'And a hundred bucks lets you tell me?'

He was cleaning his plate, mopping up fat and tomato sauce with two slices of white bread. He finished and took a long pull on his schooner.

'Why the fuck not?' he said, swallowing. 'I'll get the flick for sure from the new mob and bugger-all severance pay as a casual.'

'Who are they?'

'Consolidated Securities. Yanks. All computers and bullshit. You've run well over your twenty minutes.'

'You're looking at another hundred. Can you think of anything, an incident, something going wrong with that scam, that would've made an enemy for Patrick, supposing it got known?'

He took a chip from my plate and ate it as he thought

about an answer. He was like those people who can't think without smoking, except his prop was food.

'Three hundred,' he said.

I nodded.

He leaned closer. 'We were doing security for this pub in Hamilton. Music gig, country rock—James O'Day and the Currawongs. Well, Pat arranged for this fight to break out, nothing serious, and me and another bloke were supposed to move in and stop it. But a brazier got knocked over and a fire broke out and a good bit of the pub got burned down. Get me another drink, eh?'

I got the beer. He tapped his pocket for his cigarettes, remembered the new rules and swore.

'Go on,' I said.

'The wife of the guy who owned the pub was killed by the fire. Pat paid me a fair bit of money to keep quiet and I did, but the other bloke, the one who sort of provoked the fight, he disappeared. I heard a whisper that the pub owner killed him. Maybe Pat killed him or he just shot through. I dunno, but Pat was edgy for quite a while after.'

Pat, a killer? I wouldn't have thought so, but I was learning something new about him every day. 'This was when?'

'About two years ago.'

'The names of the other Pavee guy and the pub owner?'

He shook his head and held out his hand. 'No names.'

I gave him three hundreds but he didn't look happy. He drained his third schooner and left.

I only had to go a block to South Dowling Street and then cross to Moore Park and I fancied a contemplative walk, even though the day was cold and windy. On the paths the trees dripped on me from the morning rain and the fallen leaves were slushy underfoot. I think of myself as a summer rather than a winter person but for some reason the conditions suited my mood. I walked briskly and warmed up.

Barclay's information was interesting and would be easy enough to check, at least in its outline. I knew James O'Day, who'd fought as Jimmy O'Day, some years back. A good, careful fighter with a good, careful manager who'd picked his fights. Never won a serious title, but he'd made money and got out of the game before any damage was done and turned to his other talent—music. The Currawongs were a moderately successful band. I'd seen them live once in Bulli in the course of an investigation and talked to O'Day a few times. I owned a couple of their albums, one of them signed by James. I could ask him about the Hamilton gig and the fire and I could go there and ask questions. A man who lost a wife in a fire caused by someone playing a dodgy game might well want revenge. I felt enlivened as I went up the steep path towards the golf course. Bugger golf, I had work to do.

I phoned O'Day, spoke to one of his girlfriends, and arranged to meet him at his place in Newtown that evening. She said he was just back from a tour and was chilling. I spent part of the afternoon in the gym and the rest loading the photographs from my mobile onto the computer. I flicked through them, slotting the right paper into the printer, and printed out the shot of Patrick pretending to play his fiddle with an appropriate Dublin scene in the background—a pub. I wasn't really concentrating and was about to close down when something I'd seen in passing nagged at me.

I went through the shots more slowly until I came to the photos showing the tavern where the *céilidh* had taken place. The light wasn't the best and the pictures were fuzzy. The one of Angela Warburton in profile didn't do her justice. I found the one that had almost captured my attention—a wide-angle shot that showed Patrick with a group in the middle of a wild leap with his eyes closed in joy, and in drink. A man sitting behind him was staring at Patrick with a look of sheer malevolence on his face. He was thin, dark, not young, and not obviously one of the Travellers. Although there were other people sitting near him he gave the impression of being on his own.

I blew the image up and studied it. The hostility was unmistakable, made more emphatic by the bony thinness of his face. He had a barely touched pint of beer in front of him and a cigarette in his hand, but he didn't look drunk or as if he was about to do anything. He just stared and hated.

The next photo in the sequence was only moments later and covered the same scene, but the man was gone and Patrick had taken a breather. I ran off a copy of the photo. In the old days I'd have opened a file and the photo would have gone into it. But that was then and this was now. I pinned the *céilidh* photo and the one of Patrick with his fiddle to the corkboard in the kitchen where I could look at and think about them.

James O'Day and assorted members of the Currawongs, their road crew and girlfriends, occupied a big terrace house in Newtown close to Camperdown Park. I rolled up at about 7 pm with half a slab of beer—the acceptable calling card. A young woman let me in and took the beer. She wore modified goth gear—black clothes and shining metal—but didn't have the sullen, the-world-is-a-shitheap look. I actually got a smile.

'James is in the kitchen,' she said.

'Cooking?'

'I wish. We've got pizza coming. I thought you were it.'

'Sorry.'

She smiled again, her lip ring glinting in the light, and lifted the beer. 'You're welcome.'

I followed her down the passage past a couple of rooms, one with a whiff of marijuana leaking out. The kitchen was galley-style, made spacious by a wall being knocked out and an archway constructed. There was a big pine table in the centre and an even bigger antique oak butcher's bench along one wall. Speakers hung at various points around the room and most of the surfaces were covered with magazines, books, newspapers and CDs.

'Your visitor, James,' the woman said, 'bearing gifts.'

O'Day was in his early forties, middle-sized and lean. His Aboriginal ancestry was becoming more pronounced with the passing years. He seemed darker and heavier around the brows than when I'd last seen him. He wore a few marks of other men's fists on his face, but not many. He was sitting at the table tapping on the keyboard of a notebook computer.

'Cliff, good to see you, brother. Saw you at the Moody fight. Still interested in the sweet science, eh? This is Vicki.'

'Now and then, Jimmy. Hello, Vicki.'

She'd taken the tops off three of the stubbies in a matter of seconds. She handed me one. 'Hi, Cliff,' she said. 'Is this going to be, like, secret men's business?'

O'Day looked up from the screen, accepted the stubby and shook his head. 'Don't reckon. Hey, Cliff, what's a good rhyme for silver?'

I sat and drank. 'There isn't one.'

'No shit?' Vicki said. 'Bet there is. I'll Google it.'

O'Day laughed as she left the room. He logged off and took a swig. 'Good chick, Vic. Shit, I've got rhymes on the bloody brain. What's the reason for the very welcome visit, man?'

'D'you remember a gig you did a few years back at some pub in Hamilton? There was a fight and a fire.'

'Yeah, at the Miner's Arms. That was a bad scene. A woman

died, I heard. We got out okay, in fact we helped a few people get out.'

'Who was the owner, or the licensee?'

'One and the same—bloke named Reg Geary.'

'You had dealings with him, did you? What was he like?'

'He was a prick—very tight with a buck. We didn't get paid for the gig. That was natural, I suppose, under the circumstances. We worked there again later, but not for him.'

'How was that?'

'We did a benefit to help them raise money to rebuild the pub. Glad to do it. We had a big following there.' He took another pull on the stubby. 'Why the questions?'

'I was wondering whether he could've been responsible for something that happened here a few days ago. A mate of mine got shot.'

'In Glebe. Yeah, I read about that and saw it on the news. Didn't connect it with you, but. That's rough. Sorry. As I said, Reg was a real bastard and I know he was bitter about what happened. Not just about his wife. I heard that he'd fucked up the insurance somehow and blamed everyone but himself. He lost the pub. He might've been crazy enough to do something like that, I suppose.'

'So he's not in Hamilton anymore?'

'No, he came to Sydney. Tried to get into promotion. Hang on.'

He found his mobile under a CD and punched in some

numbers. 'Calling my agent. Hello, Gordon, James. Yeah, look, d'you know how to get in touch with Reg Geary? What? Of course I'm not wanting to work for him. Mate of mine wants to see him about something. Yeah, yeah, that right? Okay. Thanks, Gordie. See you Saturday.'

He rang off, drained his can and scribbled on the back of a magazine. 'Gordie says Geary's in a psychiatric unit in Marrickville. The cops booked him in yesterday after he assaulted a woman at some event he'd tried to promote. Here's the address.'

He tore off the corner he'd written on and handed it to me. 'A nutter. Could be your guy.'

7

You don't just wander up to a psychiatric facility, ring the bell, and ask to speak to an inmate. In the old days, when I was on passable terms with some of the police, I could've found out who arrested Geary and possibly got access to him that way. Not anymore. My doctor, Ian Sangster, wears a number of hats. I made an appointment to see him in the morning.

'Hammond Psychiatric Unit in Marrickville, Ian,' I said. 'Know it?'

'I know *of* it. I don't think you're a candidate for it quite yet.'

'Very funny. I want to talk to someone there.'

'In connection with what?'

'What else? Patrick's murder.'

'Let me make some phone calls.'

Ian got back to me a few hours later saying that he'd spoken to a doctor at the unit who was willing to allow me a short interview with Geary that afternoon, with an emphasis on the short.

'Dr Galena Vronsky,' Ian said. 'A very good clinician. Could be your type, come to think of it.'

'What did she say about Geary?'

'Nothing much, just that he's a violent paranoid schizophrenic resistant to medication. Have fun.'

Dr Vronsky was a slim, dark woman in her thirties. She was classically beautiful with violet eyes and sculptured features. She wore the standard white coat over a crisp blue blouse and a dark skirt, medium-heeled shoes. She sat me down in her office and I told her why I wanted to see Geary. I left out certain details, although there was something compelling about her and it felt almost shameful not to tell her the whole truth.

'How would you propose to go about questioning him, Mr Hardy?'

'I don't think I'll have to do much. Patrick Malloy and I were almost identical physically. If he killed Patrick and sees me he's bound to show some kind of reaction.'

'Possibly, but he's a very disturbed individual, so much so that it could be very difficult to read his reaction.'

'Do you think what I'm suggesting could do him any harm?'

She smiled and the temperature in the cold room seemed

to lift. 'I'm glad you asked that. Ian Sangster vouched for you and your stocks just went up with me. No, I don't think so. He needs detoxing and medicating, and even then . . .'

She got up. 'Come on, and don't forget I'm in control of this.'

I followed her through a series of passages with rooms on both sides. Some were open and looked more like motel rooms than cells. The place was no bedlam, closer to a sedate rest home. We passed a recreation area where a couple of men were playing table tennis while others were bent over hands of cards. Dr Vronsky opened the door to a warm, glassed-in sunroom. Three men were sitting in armchairs staring out at an expanse of grass. An orderly in a tracksuit sat in a corner working on a crossword puzzle.

Two of the men turned to look at us as we entered and one nodded a sort of greeting. The third man continued to look straight ahead. Like the others, he wore street clothes.

'This is Mr Geary,' the doctor said. 'You have a visitor, Mr Geary.'

He turned slowly and slid his chair around on the polished floor to face me. His face was deeply lined, grey-skinned and slack. His sunken eyes were blank and uninterested. 'Fuck off, shithead,' he said. 'You too, cunt.'

His hands on the arms of the chair were trembling, but as soon as he'd spoken he swivelled around and resumed his former position. I followed Dr Vronsky from the room.

She leaned against the wall, distress showing in her face.

63

'He's waiting to hear his voice. He was mildly irritated that we interrupted him.'

'He was trembling,' I said. 'This assault, what did he do?'

'He kicked a woman. Kicked her until she fell and then kicked her repeatedly. How was your cousin killed, Mr Hardy?'

'By a shotgun.'

She shook her head. 'Not possible. He has advanced Parkinson's disease. He would be quite incapable of using a firearm.'

A dead end.

'This is a damn fine instrument,' Hank said, holding up Patrick's mobile. 'It's a BlackBerry, the latest.'

'Why do they call it a blackberry? It's a noxious weed.'

'Not in the US it isn't, at least, not everywhere. Anyway, it's one word, spelled with two capital Bs.'

'What will they think of next?'

'It has a speaker phone, wireless broadband, email, huge memory, you name it.'

'So you could get up his phone numbers, his emails, photos, all that?'

'With ingenuity, yeah, in theory.'

'Meaning?'

'He uploaded almost everything to . . .'

'Where?'

Hank shrugged. 'No way to tell. A server, most likely.'

'You said almost.'

'Do you remember someone taking a picture of the two of you outside some pub or other?'

'Yeah, the Travellers Arms in Dublin. A Japanese tourist took it.'

Hank fiddled with the phone and handed it to me. 'He kept that picture, nothing else.'

I looked at the photograph. Its quality was vastly superior to any of mine. It showed us standing outside the pub; Patrick with his fiddle case under his arm and me with a rolled-up newspaper held in much the same way. For once we were wearing similar clothes dictated by the weather—jeans, sweaters and light slickers. I had a few days' stubble because my shaver had conked out, and we looked like twins again— same height, same build, same pose. I remembered that the obliging Japanese photographer had smiled and said, 'Twin brothers,' as he returned the mobile, and then, 'Brackberry,' and we'd nodded and thanked him.

I took a deep breath and put the mobile on the desk.

'If I'd been there . . .'

'You'd likely be dead,' Hank said. 'Automatic shotgun, right?'

'Yes.'

'That's a serious killing. He wasn't about to leave any witnesses. It was a Perry and Dick situation.'

Hank had just finished reading the copy of *In Cold Blood*

I'd lent him. He'd said it was one of the best books he'd ever read. I agreed.

'You're right,' I said. 'I've got to work on this.'

'Sure. I remember when you were showing me the ropes in this business and you told me to stop at every piece of information and ask yourself what conclusions to draw.'

'Okay.'

'In this case just two—the guy had something to hide and he was fond of you.'

It looked like another dead end but that often happens and you just have to scratch away until you draw blood somewhere else. I knew someone at Consolidated Securities, the firm Patrick said he was selling out to. The company was a big, international outfit, handling investigation as well as conventional security matters, and one of its policies was to mop up as many smaller operations as it could to increase market share. One technique was to recruit one-man PEAs like me. I'd been approached several times but wasn't interested. Eventually they'd get around to Hank. I phoned Bruce Carstairs, the executive who'd made the offer to me.

'Cliff Hardy,' he said and cleared his throat.

'Don't be embarrassed,' I said. 'I'm not after a job.'

As a practitioner scrubbed permanently off the books by the licensing authorities, my market value was nil. I told him I wanted some information about their acquisition of Patrick

Malloy's share in Pavee Security. Acquisition of that sort was Carstairs' area of expertise.

'Not sure I can tell you anything—commercial confidentiality and all that.'

'He was my cousin and a friend and he was shot to death in my house. I'm helping the police in their investigation and I just need to know a few things—nothing about the money.'

A pause and then he said, 'I'll help as far as I can.'

'Who was his lawyer?'

'He didn't have one. He was legally trained and did all that side of the work himself.'

'What about his bank? He must have paid the money in somewhere.'

'I see what you're getting at. No harm in telling you this, it's on the public record. There was no money involved. It was a straight share transfer—his in Pavee, and it was a substantial but not an outright majority holding, for a number of ours.'

'Can you tell me when it all went through?'

I could hear the keys clicking and remembered what Patrick had said: . . . *all computers and bullshit.* Carstairs came back on the line and gave me several dates. The last few coincided with the time of our trip.

'Emails and phone conversations to tie it up?' I said.

'Of course.'

'What about signatures?'

'All provided earlier. Look, I'm sorry . . . for your loss, but everything was perfectly straightforward. Agreement was reached easily with both parties perfectly happy.'

'Isn't that a bit unusual?'

'It's not unique. Was there anything else?'

I thanked him and rang off. He hadn't remarked on the physical similarity between Patrick and myself because we'd never met. Our dealings had been solely by phone and email.

Two days later I got a call from Dan Munro at Pavee Security. He reminded me that he'd been at the funeral and asked if I was willing for my phone number to be given to a woman named Sheila Malloy.

'Who is she?'

'She says she's Patrick's wife.'

'His wife?'

'That's what she says. I've got her on the other line, Mr Hardy, and she's very insistent.'

'Tell her I'll meet her anywhere she chooses at whatever time.'

8

I'd read that some lawyers feeling the pinch and unable to afford presentable offices were meeting their clients in Macquarie Street coffee shops, so I wasn't surprised that she proposed a cafe opposite Parliament House. Probably meant she'd have a cut-rate lawyer along. She took me at my word and set the meeting for the mid-afternoon of the same day. All this came through Munro, so I didn't even get to hear her voice and he hung up as soon as the meeting was set.

I arrived early as usual but they weren't far behind. Maybe a sign of anxiety or nervousness, maybe not. Sydney traffic being what it is, precise timing is difficult. I watched as they approached—a tall, slender woman in a dark suit and a shorter chunky man, also in a suit which, as they got closer, I could see was a three-piece pinstripe. She was smoking but dropped the butt and put her high-heeled shoe on it before reaching the outdoor table area. I stood and when she saw me she stopped in her long striding tracks and her bag fell from her shoulder.

'Jesus Christ,' she said. 'This is amazing.'

She bent to pick up her bag and her shoulder-length hair fell across her face. She swept it back and moved forward with her hand out. I took it; her nails were long and painted bright red.

'Sheila Malloy.'

'Cliff Hardy.'

'This is Harvey Spiegelman.'

'Solicitor,' he said.

I shook his hand and we sat down at the table. It was partly sheltered by a flapping canvas wall anchored to some uprights. The day was really too cool for sitting outside in comfort, but there were others at the tables for the usual reason—to smoke. Sheila Malloy took a packet of fifty from her bag and lit up. She put the packet and her lighter on the table.

A waiter came out and we ordered.

'Mrs Malloy . . .' I began.

She smiled and lines appeared on her face. She was probably on the right side of fifty, but not by much. She was good-looking in a rather narrow, thin-lipped way. Her hair was auburn; her makeup was expert. She was very vaguely familiar, but that might have been just that she looked a bit like Sigourney Weaver.

'Call me Sheila. The people at Parvee had heard from Paddy that you looked like him but they didn't tell me you were twins.'

'A genetic thing,' I said. 'We're . . . were second cousins.'

She glanced around for an ashtray and, not finding one, flicked ash on the footpath. 'Fancy that. He told me he didn't have a relative in the world.'

'He told me he was divorced.'

The coffee arrived and she used her spoon to stir the chocolate into her cappuccino. 'Well, looks like he was wrong about no relatives and I know for a fact he was lying about the divorce.'

Spiegelman leaned forward to sip at his latte, taking care to keep his silk tie out of the way. 'Sheila understands that her husband died intestate,' he said. 'Under the law, she inherits his assets.'

'That sounds right,' I said, 'if she can prove they were still married and that there's no will. That could be legally tricky, wouldn't you say?'

Sheila and Spiegelman exchanged glances. She appeared to be about to speak but he lifted his hands in a soothing gesture.

'What exactly is your interest in the matter, Mr Hardy?'

I almost laughed. I drank off the short black and waved away wisps of Sheila's smoke. 'First off, tell me why you wanted to contact me, because that's the order of things.'

Spiegelman stirred his cup. 'Well . . .'

'Don't play games with him, Harvey. When I heard Paddy was dead—'

'How did you hear?'

'From the police, of course. I don't use the name anymore but they knew how to find me. They've got us all pegged.'

I nodded. 'Right.'

'And I'll tell you something—television and crime fiction's got it all wrong. They didn't treat me as a suspect. Anyway, I got straight on to that company of his and asked a few questions. They told me nothing really, but your name came up and I remembered that you were mentioned in the paper. I wanted to know if you thought you were in line for some of his money. Is that plain enough for you?'

'That's very plain,' I said. 'And I can give you a plain answer. I don't give a stuff about his money. I'm only interested in finding out who killed him. Plain enough?'

She surprised me then with a smile that seemed to have genuine warmth in it. She put her hand on my arm, almost stroking the sleeve of my jacket. 'We're getting off on the wrong foot here, Cliff. I admit I thought you were going to turn out to be one of his rough mates from his army and drinking days. They used to show up and leech on him. But I can see that you're not like that.'

She was a chameleon. The brittle, hard-boiled manner dropped away and was replaced by something altogether more sympathetic, almost likeable.

'Of course I want to know who did such a terrible thing,'

she said, 'but I won't lie to you. Paddy treated me very badly, and he virtually robbed me. We had a house and other assets in common and when he left he managed to take them all out from under me. He was clever in the way he set everything up in his favour, under his control. He owed me and I want . . . compensation. You have to believe me.'

'I don't have to,' I said. 'None of that sounds like the Patrick I knew.'

'How long did you know him?'

She had me there. 'A matter of weeks.'

'Enough said. He had that Irish charm, a way with him, as they say.'

She had her own charm and was turning it on now, full bore. Spiegelman appeared to be taking no more than a polite interest at this point and I had to wonder what his role really was. He clicked his own lighter for Sheila as she produced another cigarette and there was no doubt; the gesture was intimate and devoted, almost embarrassing to watch.

'You weren't at the funeral,' I said.

'I didn't know about it.'

'However you look at it,' I said, 'it comes down to legalities. Is there a will? Were you divorced? Comes down to sets of papers. Have you got any?'

'I have a marriage certificate. Have you got anything?'

I couldn't help thinking of the package Patrick had posted from London. Surely not. I shrugged. 'This is of almost no interest to me. Can you throw any light on who might have wanted to kill Patrick? Kill him in that . . . emphatic way?'

'Just a minute, Hardy,' Spiegelman said. 'What are you implying?'

'Nothing,' I said. 'I'm sorry, but I don't think we can be of any use to each other. I'll pay for the coffee and be on my way. In time there'll be a niche for Patrick's ashes at Rookwood if you're interested, Sheila. I believe they keep them for a certain number of years and then dispose of them if no one claims them.'

She killed her cigarette in her coffee cup and stood. She was almost as tall as me. She blew smoke past my shoulder.

'Fuck you,' she said.

It was all getting a bit strange, out of shape. I caught a bus back to Glebe as the afternoon light died. All very well what I'd told Hank about drawing conclusions from information gained, but what if the information was highly suspect to begin with? It was Friday night with the traffic heavy and the bus losing and taking on passengers at every stop. Something was nagging at me and by the time we made the turn into Glebe Point Road I had it. The name Harvey Spiegelman rang a bell. Only faintly, but it was there. Something to follow up.

Sheila Malloy, if that's who she really was, presented a problem. I'd met women I'd found difficult to believe many times before, but she was a mixture. Her frankness about her interest in Patrick's death was one thing; her denial of their divorce was another. She used the name Paddy naturally, convincingly, but her picture of the man was very different from mine. People can change over time, but Sheila appeared to be able to change from one minute to the next.

I stopped at the Toxteth for a drink and ordered a Jamesons, Patrick's favourite tipple. I was thinking I preferred scotch when a man dropped into the chair next to mine.

'On the hard stuff, eh, Cliff?'

I knew him but couldn't immediately put a name to the face. He raised his own glass and it came to me.

'Gidday, Sammy. Good to see you again.'

Sammy Starling nodded. 'As Keef says, it's good to see you—good to see anyone.'

Sammy had been out of circulation for almost seven years, serving a sentence for manslaughter. He'd been a private detective and a good one, but a gambling problem had forced him to cross the line and become a standover man, working for gamblers. One night he went too far and the man he was putting extreme physical pressure on died. Sammy hadn't completely lost his moral bearings and he turned himself in. It was more than his life was worth to name the people he'd been working for, though that would have earned him a lesser sentence, so he served nearly the whole term. I'd put some work his way before he went off the rails, and given a character reference when he was up on the charge.

'I heard you were out,' I said, 'but I thought you were an eastern suburbs type.'

'I am. Give me Bondi any day; but I've been hanging around here hoping to see you.'

'I'm out of the business, Sammy.'

'I know that. But you always played square with me and stood up when I was in the shit, so I want to return the favour.'

I finished the whiskey and held out my glass. 'Buy me a drink and we'll call it quits.'

He dropped his voice and looked around to be sure he couldn't be overheard. 'This is serious. Do you remember Soldier Szabo?'

I nodded. Szabo was a hardcore crim who'd come after me and I'd shot and killed him in the living room of my house. Even after scrubbing at it and years of wear and tear, there was still a faint stain on the carpet where he'd bled. He was a vicious murderer and I felt no remorse, just the natural empty, stomach-churning reaction at the time.

Sammy leaned closer. 'He had a son named Frank. He was in Bathurst with me, doing time for armed robbery. He got high on ice one day and said he was going to kill the man who killed his father.'

'When was this?'

'About a year ago, bit less. I didn't think too much about it because they all go around making threats, especially when they're high, but when I heard about that bloke being killed at your place I thought I should tell you.'

I got up and bought two drinks. Sammy never drank anything but scotch and ice so I didn't have to ask. I sat down and looked at him. He was ten years younger than me and medium-sized. A welterweight, say. For someone who'd been inside for so long he looked more lined, greyer, but pretty good—he must have worked out and kept a limit on the starches.

'He's out, is he?'

'A month ago, maybe two months.'

'What's he like?'

'An animal, and a crack-head. And, Cliff, his weapon of choice was a sawn-off automatic shotgun.'

9

I'd spent a part of the previous year overseas, leaving the house in the care of a friend who'd carried out some renovations. The security system Hank Bachelor had finally persuaded me to install had malfunctioned and I hadn't got around to having it repaired. Out of the private eye business, I hadn't seen it as a priority and I had to accept that my neglect had contributed to Patrick's death. His agile killer had come in from the poorly protected back over a high fence.

Sammy Starling's information changed my thinking. In the morning I phoned Hank and asked him to come and get the system up and running again—coded alarm, sensor lights and all.

'I wondered,' Hank said. 'Didn't like to ask.'

'Yeah.'

'When do you want it?'

'Soon as you can.'

'How so, something happening?'

'No, just getting around to doing what I should've done as soon as I got back from the US trip. I've been slack.'

Maybe he believed me, maybe he didn't, but he agreed to come in the afternoon with his box of tricks. I thanked him and went to the gym where I worked out harder and longer than usual. It was a sort of useless penance. After the gym session I went to an ATM and drew out a thousand dollars and went visiting.

Ben Corbett was an ex-biker and ex-stuntman, ex because he'd crashed his bike at something like two hundred kilometres per hour and lost the use of his legs. His mates from the Badlanders motorcycle gang had looked after him by making him a sort of armourer. Corbett traded in guns for bikers and others and made some non-declarable money to top up his disability pension. He was an expert at removing serial numbers and retooling barrels, magazines and cylinders to make the weapons hard to identify. I'd encountered him when working on a blackmail case in which a movie director's wife had put her favours about with the cast and crew, including Ben. Just a memory for him now.

I drove to Erskineville where Corbett lived in a flat below street level. It was reached by a steep ramp with a bend in it that Corbett could take at full tilt in his powered wheelchair. Once a speed freak . . .

He opened the door to me and the reek of marijuana and tobacco smoke blended with the smell of gun oil and worked metal.

'Fuckin' Cliff Hardy,' he said. 'What's in the fuckin' bag?'

'A bottle of Bundy and a packet of Drum.'

'Come in, mate, come in.'

We were a long way from being mates, but I admired his resilience and courage. I'd have probably been an alcoholic mess if what happened to him had happened to me. He was killing himself with drugs and tobacco, so perhaps his apparent good humour and aggression were covers for something despairing. Impossible to say. I went down the narrow, dark passage and into the room that served as his living quarters and workshop. The flat was tiny, consisting of this room, a kitchenette and a bathroom, all fitted out for his convenience. He wheeled himself behind a workbench, where he had a rifle barrel fixed in a vice.

He produced two non-breakable glasses from under the bench and set them up. A rollie had gone out in the ashtray and he relit it with a Zippo lighter. I put the packet of tobacco next to the ashtray, ripped the foil from the bottle, pulled the cork and poured. Knowing Corbett's habits, I also had a bottle of ginger ale in the bag. I topped the glasses up, more mixer for me than him. He tossed off half of the drink and I gave him a refill.

'What can I do for youse?'

'First off, information.'

He puffed smoke, took a sip and shook his head. 'Fuckin' unlikely, but go ahead.'

'Done any work on an automatic shotgun lately? Say, sawing off, making a pistol grip?'

Corbett wore a biker beard and a bandana, concealing his receding grey hairline. The greasy remnant was caught in a ponytail tied with copper wire. The ponytail sat forward on his shoulder and it jumped back as he shook with laughter.

'Fuck you. As if I'd tell you if I had, but no. Wouldn't mind. Be a challenge. Too short and it could blow up in your face, not enough grip and you'd drop the fucker when you let loose.'

I had a drink and waited until his laughter subsided. I took the wad of notes from my pocket and fanned them. 'I need a gun.'

He pinched off the end of his rollie, picked up the packet I'd bought, took papers from the breast pocket of his flannie, expertly rolled another thin, neat cigarette and lit it.

'Like what?'

'Smith & Wesson .38 revolver.'

'You're a fuckin' dinosaur, Hardy.'

'But . . .'

'You're in luck. The Victorian cops are trading up. I can get you what you want.'

'Untraceable?'

'Yeah. What've you got there?'

'Nine hundred.'

'That'll do. How many rounds?'

'A full load.'

'Okay. Three days.'

'Two.'

'Okay.'

I took two of the notes from the wad and put them in my pocket. He took a drink and puffed on his cigarette. 'You're a bastard, Hardy.'

'I know,' I said.

Hank rang on my mobile as I left Corbett's flat. I was keeping an eye out for anything unusual—a face, a movement, a noise. I felt pretty sure that $900 would buy Corbett's cooperation, but with people caught in the criminal networks you can never be sure of their price or their other obligations.

Hank said, 'Done, front and back. Sensor lights, a siren to strip paint and a connection to the security people. Are you going to tell me why?'

'I told you.'

'You encouraged me to be persistent. I think you're lying.'

'Just send me the bill, mate, and thanks.'

I drove warily, alert to the position and speed of the cars and motorbikes around me. As far as I knew, there had never been a shooting from one moving vehicle to another in Sydney, but there's always a first time. Factor in cowboys, anxious to try what they've seen in the movies. I turned into the laneway behind my house and worked around and back up the street. Most of the parked cars were familiar and those that weren't seemed to be empty. I parked close to the house, waited and watched until two cars went harmlessly past.

I collected the mail—still nothing from the UK—keyed in the code and knew why I hadn't replaced the system. A pain in the arse. I went in and the photograph on the corkboard took my eye. The information about Frank Szabo was pushing me in another direction, into considering that the killer might've hit the wrong man by mistake. There were ways I could get a line on Szabo but it would take time. I still wasn't convinced it was the truth; the hostile stare of the man at the *céilidh* still made an impact and it was something I could follow up immediately.

I rooted through the things I'd left in my travelling bag and found Angela Warburton's card in a zipped side pocket. As she'd said, she was a photo-journalist, working for the London newspaper *The Independent* and the card carried her email address. I threw together the ingredients for chilli con carne and went upstairs to the computer while it was simmering. I emailed Ms Warburton, attached the photograph as a jpg file, and asked her if she knew anything about the man. I tossed up whether to tell her about Patrick being killed and decided not to. No point putting ideas in her head.

I washed the chilli down with Stump Jump red, watched *Lateline* on ABC, and grasped only that petrol prices were going up and no one had a clue what to do about it, and took the Hemingway I'd left behind, *Across the River and Into the Trees*, up to bed. It didn't hold me. I slept poorly. I dreamed of Lily and woke up early needing a piss and aching from the sensation of having had her in dreamland and losing her when my eyes were open.

Angela Warburton's reply was there when I logged on in the morning:

Cliff
Sorry you didn't look me up in London. We could've compared surfing notes. I'm guessing you were a surfer. We do it here on the Cornish coast and it's not too bad. Anyway, since you're all business, the guy in the photo is Sean Cassidy and he's a bit of a mystery man. He's a Traveller, that's for sure, but they say he doesn't quite belong. A military background of some kind, I learned. Paddy Malloy agreed to let me do a photo piece on his family and Cassidy fought him every inch of the bloody way. This is all after you two left. In the end it didn't work out. They're a fractious lot, which was interesting, but it wasn't worth the grief. I didn't get enough shots to make a worthwhile piece, and most of the people clammed up once the clannish shit hit the fan.
That's it. I'm back in London and the offer still stands.
Go well,
Angie

I didn't like the sound of that. A military background

suggested the IRA or the Ulster lot, murderous bastards both, at their worst. Surely Patrick hadn't involved himself in that crazy sectarian business. The trouble was, the more I found out about him the more I realised that I hadn't really known him at all.

I replied to Angela, thanking her and saying I didn't know when I was next likely to be in London, but extending a similar invitation to her in Sydney. It felt vaguely ridiculous, having a penpal at my age, but there was something comforting about it as well.

Nothing much to do except wait for the packages from the UK. A search for Frank Szabo would have to stay on hold until I had the gun. It was still dark outside and I fooled around with the alarm, making sure that the sensor lights worked and that I knew how to deactivate the system and keep the code in my head separate from my PIN and the other numbers we live by these days.

I took my meds, poached two eggs and ate them and collected the paper. I was on my second cup of coffee and reading through the letters when the doorbell sounded. Unlikely that Frankie Szabo would ring the bell. Maybe it was the overseas packages—they wouldn't fit in the letterbox and the postie sometimes took the trouble to ring before dumping them on the doorstep. I used the peephole: my visitor was Sheila Malloy.

10

I opened the door.

'Good morning,' she said. 'Surprised?'

'Very.'

I stepped back and she came in. She was wearing a navy pants suit in some silky material with a short jacket that emphasised the length of her legs and her height. Her hair had a bronze shimmer in the early morning light. Her suede bag and shoes matched her suit. She looked confident, relaxed and healthy, as though she'd slept well.

'There's more to talk about,' she said as we moved down the passage.

'Is there?'

She stopped when she reached the living room and took in the well lived-in décor. 'You don't like me, do you?'

'I don't know you. Impossible to say.'

'Do I smell coffee?'

I waved towards the kitchen and we went through. There was enough coffee in the percolator for a couple of cups. I got another cup from the cupboard and poured.

'Milk?'

'Please.'

'Be a bit cool.'

'Microwave it. I'm not a purist.'

I smiled at that. I freshened my cup, added milk to hers, and put both in the microwave. She sat at the bench in the breakfast nook and I waited to hear the cigarettes come out and the click of the lighter. Didn't happen.

'Very domesticated,' she said. 'You live alone?'

'Sometimes.'

She laughed. 'I'm glad Paddy had a mate . . . at the end. He wasn't good at keeping friends and mostly they weren't worth keeping.'

I brought the cups over and sat. 'How did you find me, Sheila?'

'Come on, anyone can find anyone these days, you should know that. But there's no mystery—my agent knows you.'

'Agent?'

'Belinda O'Connell. You contacted her to trace some actor you were after. I'm an actress—actor, as we have to say these days.'

Maybe that accounted for the changeability. It did for the familiarity. I realised that I'd seen her in an ABC TV series with a legal theme that had held Lily's and my attention for a few episodes. And I recalled that Harvey Spiegelman had plated a minor part as a lawyer. She smiled as she saw recognition dawn on me. She got up and struck a pose, leaning on the bench.

'The prosecution is tilting at windmills . . .'

I drank some coffee and nodded. She sat down and stirred her coffee. 'Yeah, the poor woman's Sigourney Weaver.'

'You weren't Malloy then. But Harvey, I remember, was still Spiegelman.'

'Right. Sheila Lambert, stage name. I've fallen on hard times since then. There aren't many parts for women with years on the clock. Harvey's doing it tough, too. He was never much of a lawyer or an actor and I just brought him along to our meeting for ballast.'

'You're not smoking.'

'I'm quitting.'

I wondered if that was true or just part of the act for today. She leaned forward to push her cup away on the table and the top of her jacket gaped open. She wasn't wearing a blouse or a bra and I could see the shape of her small, firm breasts. I'd been celibate for longer than I cared to remember and I felt a stirring. I couldn't tell whether the movement was a come-on or not, but she surprised me with what she said next.

'I want to see where he died.'

'For Christ's sake, why?'

She shrugged; I tried not to look, but the movement stiffened her nipples under the tight jacket.

'The man was a huge part of my life and he damaged me. I damaged him, too. Call it closure. D'you think that's sick?'

I was aroused and confused. I stood and she slid out from her seat and moved towards me, touching my arm.

'Show me.'

We went through the door to the back bathroom. I'd had it cleaned, hadn't replaced the shower curtain, but some of the rings still hung there. Patrick's head and body had taken the full force of the blasts but there were a few chips on the tiles where stray pellets had struck. The space was white, sterile, dead—no blood, no bone, no tissue. Nothing.

She leaned against me. 'I thought I'd feel something but I don't. This is creepy. You look so much like him and I loved him so much for so long. Off and on, I mean. God, I'm going to end up telling you my life story.'

The hard shell had well and truly cracked and for a minute we stood still. I was thinking about Patrick and I was sure she was, too. I guided her back to the kitchen.

'I'm a good listener,' I said. 'Look, would you like a drink? A toast to Patrick? It's a bit early but . . .'

She smiled and stayed close to me. 'It's later somewhere. I'd like that. It's been a while since I drank wine in the morning but why not? I wish . . .'

'What?'

'I was going to say I wish I'd met you before Paddy. What a dumb thing to say. Sorry.'

I got a bottle of white from the fridge and poured. We both sat and touched glasses without speaking. She took a decent slug of the wine and smiled at me. She had small, even teeth and her eyes crinkled with the smile. She did everything gracefully and I wanted badly to touch her. I was suddenly aware of my scruffy appearance.

'I'm glad you came,' I said. 'Hard to put it into words, but . . .'

'Try, why don't you?'

I reached out and covered her smooth hand with my battered paw. We stood. I knocked my glass over and the wine spilled. I put my arms around her. We stood in a tight embrace. I thought I could hear her heart pounding. I could definitely feel mine.

She said, 'I thought I came just to talk, but now I'm not sure. Without knowing it I think maybe I came for this.' She pressed close against me and her hand went down to my erection.

We made love in the tangled sheets and blankets I'd left after my sleepless night. Her body was smooth, lean and pale and she was athletic and inventive with it. I found myself almost fighting to get my share of the pleasure and we were sweaty and panting when she shoved a pillow under her rump and pulled me down and into her. We fucked hard, and I don't know who came first. We rolled apart, gasping. Sweat beaded her upper lip and I wiped it off with a finger.

She laughed. 'Yes, that happens when it's good. Not very chic.'

'Chic's overrated.'

She traced the scar line from my bypass, not much more now than a series of discolourations. 'There's a difference. Shit, I didn't mean . . .'

'It's okay. We were both in the grip of something a bit weird.'

'Are you sorry?'

'No.'

The room was cold. The heat we'd generated was fading and I clawed up the sheet, jerked the blanket free of the tangle and covered us. The desire she'd triggered in me was still there and I pulled her close and wrapped my arms around her. She felt my unshaven chin.

'I'm glad you hadn't shaved,' she said. 'I'm going to have bristle rash, but I can look at it and tell myself I've had a top fuck from someone who wanted it as much as I did.'

We showered, separately, in the upstairs bathroom, got dressed and went back to the kitchen. By now it was later in the morning, late enough to have another go at the white wine. The day had improved during our lovemaking, and we took the drinks out into the courtyard where we could sit comfortably in the patch of sun protected from the wind.

I told Sheila what I'd learned about the dodgy dealings of Pavee Security and the dead end I'd struck there and with the company that had bought his shares.

'Sorry to tell you,' I said, 'but there was no money involved. Just a share transfer.'

'But the shares are worth money. Sorry to sound so mercenary, but I think I'm entitled. He was a psychological mess when he came back from that ridiculous soldier of fortune episode, and I just about supported him through university. Then he upped and left.'

'Why?'

'He became successful with his property developments. He still needed me for a while because it was edgy stuff— juggling loans and contracts, dealing with unions and politicians—but when it all sorted out and the money came in, he didn't need me anymore. I think he associated me with his earlier struggles.'

'Why didn't you divorce him and get a share of the assets then?'

She sipped her drink and shivered. I went inside and got a jacket, the one Patrick had borrowed as it happened, and draped it round her shoulders. Our hands touched as she drew it closer.

'Thanks. It's nice out here. I was busy then and doing pretty well. I thought it might work out. Then I went to America for a while and bombed. I lost touch with him and I was hitting the booze pretty hard. I was . . . ashamed.'

I could understand that. In my experience, at those low ebb points you can still maintain some pride even though it's not in your best interest. It feels like all you have left.

We were sitting side by side on a seat I'd constructed out of stacked bricks and pine planks—the limit of my skills. I put my arm around her shoulder and she stiffened.

'Do you believe me about not being divorced?'

'I want to say yes.'

'Jesus, an honest man. Let me show you something.'

She got up and went into the house. I watched her elegant strut on her high heels and knew all my impulses were affected by the sexual experience and a hope for more. She came back and handed me a photograph. It showed a man and a woman outside the Sydney Registry Office. Patrick, in a stylish dark suit, was looking at Sheila as if he wanted to make love to her right there on the steps. She, in a low-necked sheath dress and carrying flowers, looked as if she'd oblige. Another couple, presumably their witnesses, looked almost embarrassed in the presence of such overt sexuality.

Sheila came closer, took my hand and locked it between her thighs.

'You'd have looked just like that back then, wouldn't you, Cliff?'

'Never had a suit that good.'

She laughed. We kissed and went back upstairs to do it again.

11

Sheila asked me if I knew anything about making a claim against an estate where there was no will. 'I think the spouse automatically inherits.'

'You said Paddy told you we were divorced.'

'Right.'

'He might've told other people the same. That could . . . complicate things.'

'Would Harvey be up to sorting it out?'

She shook her head and I gave her the name and number of my solicitor, Viv Garner, who I thought could advise her.

We were downstairs, behaving slightly awkwardly. She'd told me she was sharing a flat in Balmain but didn't say who with. She gave me her mobile number but not the address. I gave her my number.

'I've got a couple of auditions to go to over the next few

days. I'll try to see Mr Garner and I'll give you a call if I learn anything useful.'

'Call me anyway.'

We moved down the passage.

'What will you be doing, Cliff?'

'Still poking around to see if I can find out who killed him.'

We got to the door, reached for each other and kissed hard. She moved her head until her mouth was close to my ear. Her hair smelled just faintly of tobacco smoke.

'Is that dangerous?'

'I hope not.'

'But you'll do it anyway.'

'Don't you want . . . justice?'

She shook her head. 'I've done a bit of Shakespeare in my time. He didn't believe in justice and neither do I . . . I only want for you not to be hurt.'

It was mid-afternoon and cool again as the shadows lengthened. She was driving a tired red Beetle. She revved it hard and took off slowly, smokily. I stood on the pavement and watched the car out of sight. I wanted to believe all she said, but I remembered how differently she'd appeared at first and that she was an actress. She hadn't told me her address; but then, I hadn't told her I was waiting for Patrick's package from the UK.

I rummaged through one of the cardboard boxes I keep old files in until I found the one involving Soldier Szabo. He was a career criminal, a standover man, hired by a developer who'd run into some trouble with people trying to protect old buildings. Szabo'd exceeded his brief and killed two people and would've killed me if I hadn't got lucky. I looked through the notes to see if there was any useful information about him. Not much, other than that he had a wife and a flat in Norton Street, Leichhardt. That was the best part of twenty years ago, but some people stay put. Like me.

My useful contacts in the RTA, the police and the parole services had gone along with my PEA licence. Those contacts had made locating people a lot easier than it would be now. There were too many Szabos in the telephone directory to make that useful, and none in Leichhardt. The only thing to do was ask around—risky because word could get back. Before I could do that I needed the gun.

The excitement Sheila Malloy had caused was ebbing, but I found it difficult to think of anything else or to concentrate on other matters. Too restless to read, didn't want to hang around Megan and Hank, a bit too early for serious eating and drinking. I realised that I hadn't checked the mail and when I did I found two cards advising of parcels to be collected at the post office—one for Patrick and one for me. I'd seen Patrick's signature on his passport and when he'd signed traveller's cheques and I forged it on his card, nominating myself as his agent. Remembering that my package of books was weighty and Patrick's had looked much the same, I drove rather than walked to the post office as usual. I presented the cards and my ID and collected the parcels.

I had no reason to think Patrick's parcel contained anything of particular interest but, unlike me, he'd paid hefty insurance on it and had sealed it more carefully and with heavier tape. But I'm slack about such things. I opened the long blade on my Swiss army knife and started on the job of cutting the tape on the postpack.

I freed the flap, lifted it and emptied the contents out onto the kitchen bench. There were a couple of books—guides to Irish sights and scenes and a hardback map, a book of instruction for fiddle players, and a boxed miniature chess set. Patrick had tried to teach me the game during a dull time waiting for a flight but I'd proved unteachable. There was a surprising amount of packing, in the form of sheets from the *London Times*. I put the box aside and noticed that it didn't rattle as it always had when he'd handled it. I undid the clasp. Inside, instead of the chess pieces, was a heavily taped package about the size of a couple of cigarette packets.

The doorbell rang and for a moment I thought it might be Sheila, abandoning her audition calls and coming back to carry on where we'd left off. But the peephole showed me that it was a man wearing a suit and a serious expression. I opened the door.

'Cliff Hardy?'

'That's right.'

He held up his warrant card and produced a document he unfolded and waved in front of me.

'I have a warrant to search these premises on the grounds of suspicion of the importation of illicit items, as specified in the Customs Act.'

part two

12

They read me my rights and then it was back to Surry Hills again. I knew I was in trouble. My standing with the police, never high, these days was positively poor. They had me red-handed for forging a name and opening a package not addressed to me. The fact that Patrick had been murdered in my house didn't help. Their behaviour would depend very much on what the illicit substance was, and I had no idea.

I was ushered into an interview room and left for the best part of an hour. Standard procedure, but I knew they'd be digging out bits of paper and talking to people like the cop in charge of the investigation into Patrick's death. I struggled to remember his name. In the past I'd have entered it in the notebook for the case I was working on. Not now. Trying to remember the name gave me something to do. I tried the usual tricks: visualising the person; running through the alphabet hoping a letter would trigger the memory. My mental image of him was too vague to be helpful. I got it on the third run-through—W for Welsh, Detective Inspector. First name forgotten, but that didn't matter. They'd be talking to him for sure, and he'd remember that I'd said nothing about parcels coming from the UK.

If I'd been expected to read the name on the arresting officer's warrant card, I hadn't: I'd been given no names since. When he came back into the room and turned on the recording equipment, I saw that he was looking nervous, fumbling the switches. I hadn't noticed it before in the surprise and the speed of the proceedings, but he was young.

He settled in a chair a metre away from mine with a small metal desk between us. He looked at me, swore and left the room, coming back a minute or two later with a file. He opened it and cleared 'Interview with . . .'

'You haven't turned on the recorder,' I said. 'Light's not showing.'

He had the misfortune to have a fair complexion, which showed his blush. He switched on the recorder and cleared his throat. With his hand on the file, he began again.

'Interview with Mr Cliff Hardy by Acting Detective Sergeant Kurt Reimas, Surry Hills . . .'

He stated the date and looked up.

'I'm not saying a word without my lawyer being present.'

'That can be arranged, of course,' he said. 'But I'd encourage you to cooperate in this preliminary interview . . .'

I shook my head. 'I've been through this many times, *Acting* Sergeant. Not another word.'

What I said seemed to encourage him. He closed the file and turned off the recorder. 'I'm sure you have,' he said. 'Served a sentence at Berrima, I see, stripped of an investigator's licence . . . but things have changed. You can be held for some time now without charge or access to legal advice.'

'To do with terrorism.'

He smiled. 'That's subject to wide interpretation. You've recently returned from overseas in the company of a person who has been murdered in a brutal manner, and you've been found in possession of an imported illicit substance. Do you want to reconsider?'

'No.'

They took me to the lock-up and put me in an observation cubicle, one of a set, with a perspex wall and a heavy metal door. Nothing there but a cement bench to sit on and a metal toilet. I was the only resident. I knew this had to be temporary. If the intention was to keep me for days this wouldn't do. You couldn't sleep there. It was meant to scare me but it didn't; I'd been in worse places.

After a few hours I was moved to a cell with a washbasin, a toilet and a set of metal bunks. A man was lying on the top bunk. He sat up as I came in and his head almost hit the low roof.

'Got a smoke, mate?' he said.

'No. Sorry.'

'Fuck.' He lay back down and those were the only words I ever heard him speak.

I sat on the bunk and prepared myself for a long wait. I doubted that Reimas would try to invoke the terrorism provisions against me. It'd be a thin case and, after recent failures, the police would be wary of taking that course. It might have been different if the substance was anthrax or something similar, but I couldn't see Patrick as a terrorist. Heroin or cocaine were more probable, I supposed, but the UK didn't seem a likely source. Also, the terrorism accusation meant involving the federal police, something state cops were always reluctant to do. Sooner or later they'd have to charge me and take me before a magistrate. Couldn't do that without allowing me legal representation.

It was a long night. My companion snored and coughed and climbed down three or four times to piss. Prostate trouble and emphysema. At 6 am a Corrective Services officer told him he was going to Parramatta. He groaned and took one last intermittent, trickling piss and was gone.

Ten minutes later I was given a cup of tea and two slices of toast, both cold. I ignored them. I'd missed my evening and morning meds. I didn't think that would do me any great harm, but I disliked the feeling of dependency. By ten o'clock the inactivity and lack of human interaction were eating at me. I felt dishevelled and dirty after sleeping in my clothes. I hadn't shaved for forty-eight hours and my face itched. I was thinking of asking for a razor when I was handed a mobile phone.

'You look dreadful,' Viv Garner said.

We were in an interview room like the one I'd been in before except there was no recording equipment and we both had cups of reasonably acceptable coffee.

'I'm not at my best,' I said, but in fact I felt all right, mostly due to relief at being, if not at liberty, not in a cell.

'I thought when you were . . . forcibly retired, things would calm down. But here we are again.'

'Keeps you on your toes.'

'Don't joke, Cliff. This could be serious.'

'What was in the chess box?'

'Steroids. Powerful steroids with built-in masking agents. State of the art or better. Highly illegal. Worth a fortune.'

'What about this terrorism stuff?'

'Bluff, to scare you.'

'They can't think I had anything to do with steroids.'

'You're a gym goer and you've had a bypass. You could be looking to regain your former fitness.'

'Bullshit.'

'Cliff, they've got you forging a signature and opening another person's mail. And they're talking about a withholding evidence charge—your old bugbear.'

I knew what he meant, the failure to tell Welsh about the packages posted from London, and a charge I'd once been convicted on.

'That's thin though, isn't it? I could say I didn't know about them, or I forgot.'

107

Viv shook his head. 'For some reason, God knows why, they must've tracked the parcels. I'm betting they know the stuff was posted from the same place at the same time. You didn't know much about this cousin of yours, did you?'

'That's putting it mildly. Has Sheila Malloy, his wife, been in touch?'

'She has, and it's another thing that doesn't look good if it became known. I only spoke with her on the phone, but from the way she sounded, I'm guessing—'

'All right, all right. What are they more interested in—nailing me on these Mickey Mouse charges or finding out who killed Patrick?'

As soon as I said that I saw the connection. If Patrick was involved in a lucrative steroid racket and hadn't given satisfaction, he could have been a target. But you'd expect a bashing or a wounding, not a brutal killing. But then, there was always 'roid rage to consider.

'Both,' Viv said.

'So what's likely to happen now?'

Viv checked his watch. 'We're due for a magistrate hearing in twenty minutes. You'll be charged with illegal importation and possession, with other charges pending. I'll reserve the right not to enter a plea until a full charge with evidence is forthcoming.'

I'd been through it before and had lost, but that time I was guilty as sin. 'Then what?'

'I'll apply for bail. The police won't oppose it because

they want you on the loose, but on a chain to see if you lead them somewhere more important. My guess is—surrender of passport and fifty thousand surety.'

'I can make that,' I said, 'thanks to Lily. And I wasn't planning on going anywhere.'

We went up before the beak in Liverpool Street and it worked out pretty much as Viv said. I agreed to hand my passport in at the Glebe station and to report there each week. I signed a document pledging my security and that was it. The police prosecutor appeared to be just going through the motions.

'What about Sheila?' I asked Viv when we were outside the court.

'She has no problem, unlike you. All she has to do is apply to the Probate Office for Letters of Administration. Once granted, that ensures her right to the estate.'

'Did she tell you that Patrick said they were divorced?'

'She did. Again, that's pretty simple. Divorce proceedings are a matter of public record. She initiates a search to support her contention. She probably doesn't even have to do that if no other claims are made. If another claim is made what Patrick told you becomes relevant, but I don't suppose you'd want to bring that up. Am I right?'

'I'm not sure.'

We were in George Street, heading for a bus stop. Like me, Viv saw public transport as the only sensible way to get around in the city. Unlike me, he had a Seniors card. When we reached the bus stop he gave me a searching look.

'You don't believe her?'

'I don't know. I *want* to believe her.'

He shook his head. 'You have a knack for trouble on several fronts.'

A Leichhardt bus that'd get us both close to where we wanted to go arrived and we caught it. At that time of day it was only half full and we were able to talk without annoying anyone or being overheard.

'Can Sheila jump through those legal hoops herself?'

'She could, but it'd be better to get a solicitor—quicker, easier.'

'And more expensive.'

'Not very. Look at me, I'm travelling by bus.'

'You've got a Beemer at home. Did she ask you to act for her?'

'An old one. Yes, she did, but I declined. I'm not taking on new clients, Cliff. My wife won't let me, and I've got all the hassles I need with the few I've got. I'll send you an invoice.'

I got off in Glebe Point Road. The pub beckoned but a shower and a change of clothes beckoned more. There's something about Corrective Services sleeping quarters, and I've been in a few, that seems to taint your clothes, your hair, your skin. I went home, stripped off, showered and shaved and dressed in clothes that were moderately fresh. I've always liked Nick Nolte's line in *Forty-Eight Hours*, when his girlfriend hands him his shirt after she's been wearing it and he puts it on to go to work. She says, 'If you'd let me sleep over at your place you could at least go to work in a clean shirt.' Nolte says, 'What makes you think there's any clean shirts at my place?'

I had clean shirts but what was making me think of movies, actors? Sheila.

13

With his apparent involvement in steroid smuggling and my uncertainty about Sheila's game—she wouldn't be the first to arrange the convenient death of a spouse with money as the motive—it looked increasingly as though Patrick was the true target for the man with the shotgun. But the threat from Frank Szabo couldn't be ignored.

The possession of an unlicensed handgun is a serious offence and with my record almost certainly meant jail time. And for someone on bail with heavy charges pending, it would compound the trouble. I had no choice, but I took Viv's warning about possible police surveillance on board and arranged for Hank to check my landline for bugs. I bought a new mobile phone in a Telstra shop—new SIM card, new account, new number. If the powers that be could monitor mobiles as they can in the movies, they'd get only innocuous stuff from my old mobile. Anything important or potentially incriminating I'd reserve for my new phone.

The first call I made was to Sheila. I left a message that she should only call me on the new number. It felt like paranoia, but paranoia can be protective. Ever since the initial suspension of my licence, the subsequent cancellation, denial of my appeal and lifelong ban, I'd felt threatened. I'd played fast and loose with the authorities for many years and there were some policemen and bureaucrats who would have loved to even the score. I booked the Falcon into a garage for an unnecessary service and hired an anonymous Toyota Camry. I drove to Erskineville to visit Ben Corbett.

'Ex-police,' Corbett said, handing me the pistol. 'Must've got lost somehow. Mint condition. Only ever fired on the fuckin' range and not much then. All identification removed. Barrel retooled. Fully loaded with first class ammo. Yours for twelve hundred.'

I put the weapon down and gave him the extra money. 'You're a crook.'

'That's right, and now so are you.'

I examined the .38; broke it open, removed the cartridges, spun the cylinder and sighted down the barrel. What Corbett said was true. The pistol hadn't seen any serious action and I hoped it would stay that way. The twelve hundred dollars implied an unspoken contract—Corbett would never tell anyone that he'd supplied me with the gun and, if I got caught with it, I'd never reveal the source. Doing deals with criminals isn't comfortable, but sometimes there's no other way. Nobody knows that better than the cops and the lawyers.

I still had the chamois leather shoulder holster I'd used when I was licensed to carry a firearm and I'd worn it to the meeting. I slipped the pistol into it and adjusted the holster with a shoulder shrug I'd done a hundred times before, but not lately.

Corbett grinned as he relit one of the extinguished rollies wedged around the sides of his ashtray. 'Small of the back's better.'

'If you want to shoot yourself in the arse.'

'Goodbye, Hardy. If I never fuckin' see you again it'll be too fuckin' soon.'

'That's no way to talk. I'll be right here to sell it back to you when I finish this little bit of business.'

'It'll cost you.'

'Everything does, Ben, everything does.'

Then it was a matter of doing the rounds to get a line on Frank Szabo. It meant the outlay of a fair bit of money and the consumption of a fair amount of alcohol. The money wasn't a problem but the booze was. The last thing I needed was to be picked up for DUI with an illegal pistol under my arm. That was a sure way to go where Frank had recently been. So I had to take it in stages and spread the work out over a couple of days.

If Frank Szabo had been after me he'd know by now that he'd killed the wrong man. If he was as psychopathic as his father it wouldn't bother him too much and he'd stick around for another try. It was an uncomfortable feeling but I had one thing in my favour—to kill with a shotgun you have to get close. On the evidence of Patrick's murder, the killer *wanted* to be close to see the results of his work. I'd done some sniping in the army and it's basically a mathematical business: adjust the weapon for range, trajectory and terrain; allow for wind, fix the target in the crosshairs and fire. You hit or you miss and that's that. You take the emotion out of it if you can. If you can't, you're not a sniper. I was for a while; then I wasn't.

These days, you don't go looking for underworld people by asking questions in pubs, clubs, brothels or at racetracks. The old days when they accumulated at defined and known places are gone. They disappeared in Sydney some time back, lingered on in Melbourne through the gangland wars, but now respectability rules. But some things remain the same. The underworld is as riven with competition, vindictiveness and payback as politics, and there is no loyalty that money won't overcome. Fear is a factor though, and it's best to have it on your side.

I trawled through the people I knew—the ones I'd met in jail and in the course of my work; the ones who'd come to me with information in the past and the ones I'd had to handle when all they wanted was to crack my skull. Some I liked, some I almost liked, most I disliked intensely. I met them in offices, in restaurants, in pubs, in hospitals and a couple in jail visits. It was like panning for gold with nothing showing. Then there was a nugget in the form of Marvis Marshall.

Marshall, an African American, had come to Australia in the eighties to play basketball for the Sydney Kings. He'd played a season or two in the American league but hadn't made the grade and Australia offered him a chance to play successfully at a lower level. He did well for a season, injured his knee as so many do and that was the end of his career down under. During the year he'd met and married an Australian woman and had a child, so his citizenship was assured. In retirement, he operated for a while as a player agent and manager but suspicion arose about him attempting to influence players to tank games and he was warned off the basketball scene.

At 199 centimetres and a hundred kilos going up, he was scary big and he found work as a bouncer and enforcer for gamblers and a car repossesser for some of the more dubious dealers. He was charged with assault several times but evaded conviction by intimidating witnesses. His bad character was equalled only by his charm and I had got, warily, to know him, at the Redgum Gym in Leichhardt where he lifted weights with the pin in the bottom slot. After those he'd known in Chicago and Detroit, he had contempt for Sydney crims. He made fun of them and would tell tales about them if he was in the mood and the beer was flowing.

I'd been looking out for him for a few days during my own workouts and eventually he turned up. He was running to fat but still awesomely powerful. He saw me going through my middle-of-the-range workout and beckoned me over to the bench press stand.

'Hey, Cliff, my man. Spot me?'

He meant stand by and help if the weight attempted proved too much for him or if he faltered for some reason. This was a ridiculous request given the difference in our strength and he knew it.

'Don't be silly,' I said. 'If you can't handle it I couldn't and you're looking at a crushed chest.'

'Piker,' he said, as he loaded weights onto the bar.

'Tell you what I will do,' I said. 'I'll buy you a few schooners in return for a chat.'

'You're on, man. Stand aside. I got testosterone to burn.'

He went into his routine, muscles and veins in his head and torso bulging and sweat breaking out all over his big, brown body. It made me tired to watch him. I finished my stint, showered, and waited for him in the foyer. He came bounding out dressed in his usual tight T-shirt, hooded jacket, jeans and basketball boots. But the outfit was shabby and some flab was moving on his torso. Marvis's best days were behind him.

We crossed to the pub on the corner of Carlisle Street and

I ordered two schooners of old for him and one of light for me. He put the first drink down in a couple of gulps, sighed and settled back in his creaking chair.

'So, Cliff, I hear you had a bout with the big C.'

'No, with a heart attack, and I won.'

He patted the roll of fat around his waist. 'Headed that way myself less'n I make some changes.'

'I'm looking for someone.'

He smiled. 'Ain't we all?'

'Frankie Szabo.'

'Don't know why anyone would be looking for him. He's a mean mother.'

'I know that. I have my reasons.'

He held out his empty glass. 'Which are?'

I shook my head and got up to get him another drink. My glass was half full, but when I got back he'd emptied it.

'Savin' you from yourself, brother. Why I'm asking is that I can see that you're carrying and I like to know what I'm selling and why.'

I was wearing a loose denim jacket that I thought concealed the shoulder holster, but Marvis's eyes were sharpened by experience.

'It's for protection, nothing more.'

'Yeah, sure. I'm just a dumb nigger doesn't know nothing.'

'Don't come that line with me.' I pulled a newspaper cutting, a bit frayed now from constant use, about Patrick's death, from my pocket and passed it to him. I told him the dead man and I were related, that we looked alike and the killing happened in my house.

Marvis whistled. 'I get it.'

'I never thought you were dumb, Marvis.' I took out my wallet and peeled off two hundred dollar notes and one fifty. 'For the pleasure of your company. Same again if you can help.'

'You trust me?'

'No.'

'Good. I don' trust folks as trust me.'

I put the notes under my empty glass. 'Szabo. He was in your line of work but he expanded a little which put him inside.'

'Dumb, and him not even a nigger.'

'Marvis.'

'Happens I did run into someone who ran into Frankie recently. Sold him certain items, he said.'

'What items?'

'Didn't say, but this man deals in what you might call ordnance and mind-altering substances.'

'Great. Who are we talking about?'

'Nobody you know or want to know, but he told me a bit about Frankie's new . . . field of endeavour. Seems he joined a certain organisation. Another two-fifty you said?'

'For something solid that checks out.'

Marvis slid the now damp notes towards him and

beckoned with his index finger. I took out more money and leaned closer across the table.

Marvis smiled and chuckled like Gene Hackman. 'Frankie's in with a soldier of fortune crew, name of the Western Warriors up Hawkesbury way. Ain't hard to find—fuckers have themselves a website.'

14

I was heading for home and my Mac when Sheila called on my mobile. Mindful of my precarious legal position, I pulled over to take the call.

'Where are you?' she said.

'Almost home.'

'Can I visit? I've got something to celebrate.'

She was waiting out front when I arrived. She put her arms around me and we kissed. Then she pulled back, pointing to my armpit.

'Is that what I think it is?'

'For protection only. Come in and tell me what's happened.'

I thought it was going to be something legal—applying for the document Viv had mentioned, or a positive result from the divorce records search, but her manner and her clothes told me something different. She was wearing a blue silk dress with a faux fur jacket. She'd had something done to her hair and her shoes looked new. She moved with the same grace as before but perhaps more confidently. No whiff of tobacco smoke. She produced a bottle of champagne from her bag and waved it in my face.

'I got the part.'

Her face was alight with happiness and it communicated directly to me. I reached for her and we kissed again. It had been a long time since I'd had what has to be one of the great human experiences—the blending and sharing of sexual and emotional and professional pleasure. It had happened a few times before—when Lily won a Walkley award for journalism; when Glen Withers got a police promotion; when Helen Broadway's vineyard scored a gold medal; when Cyn had got a commission to design a building. I hadn't expected to feel it again, but here it was.

We opened and poured and drank. She told me about the role in the film she'd auditioned for—the avenging mother in a thriller about a miscarriage of justice. She said she needed to project sex and danger and cracked it at the audition.

'I have to thank you, Cliff.'

'How's that?'

'You supplied the sex charge and you still aren't sure that I didn't arrange to have Patrick killed, are you?'

I'd taken off my jacket, removed the shoulder rig, stowed it away, and taken out the notebook I'd opened just that morning to keep track of what I was doing. My habit was to write down the names of the people I was dealing with under the case heading and draw connecting arrows and dots between them indicating possible guilt, possible lies, gaps in information. I showed her the dotted lines running from her name.

'What's that mean?'

'What you said—a maybe.'

'What's this?'

I'd drawn a line through the information about James O'Day, the fire at the hotel in Hamilton, and the aggrieved publican.

'No connection,' I said. I was high on adrenalin and alcohol. 'Case closed.'

'But not for me?'

'Not yet.'

We made love. It was slower this time but just as good. Only other difference was that she was careful with her clothes— new underwear, too. Amazing what a change a bit of good luck can make. She didn't even mention the legal advice she'd had from Viv until after we'd dressed and were thinking of where to go for dinner. We agreed on walking to the Indian in Glebe Point Road.

'Your lawyer mate was helpful,' she said.

'Done anything about it yet?'

'No, but on the strength of this job I'll be able to get

someone good, not poor old Harvey. What have you been doing with yourself?'

I told her about my possible nemesis, Szabo, and the reason for carrying the gun. Didn't mention the parcels from the UK or the night in the lock-up. She smoothed down her dress and glanced at the cupboard where I'd put the pistol.

'Are you going to take it with you now?'

'No.'

'Why not?'

I shook my head, didn't want to go into the details.

'Might help me to get in character,' she said. 'Sorry, I know it's serious. That's the trouble with this business, confusing make-believe with reality.'

I thought about that as we walked. She took my arm proprietorily. With her height, stylish clothes and gleaming hair, she turned heads. *Was this make-believe or reality?* We all play roles, but actors can play them more convincingly than most.

I ate my fill; she ate much less.

'Have to watch my figure. This bitch I'm playing's thin as a snake, acts like one, too. Have to do some jogging, which I hate. What d'you do to the keep the flab down?'

'Gym, walking, bit of tennis. Light on the carbs.'

She pointed to my plate. 'I didn't notice.'

'You ate so little I didn't want them to think we didn't enjoy the meal.'

We walked back briskly against a cold wind. We turned

into my street and she stopped. 'I'm parked just here, Cliff. Do you want me to stay the night?'

I put my arm around her. 'I insist.'

I turned on a couple of heaters and made coffee while she wandered around looking at the books, the DVDs and CDs. She examined the photograph of Lily I had propped up on a shelf but made no comment. She went over to the corkboard and stopped in her tracks. She pointed to the photograph of the malevolent Sean Cassidy at the *céilidh*.

'Jesus Christ, what's this doing here?'

I poised the plunger over the coffee. 'It was taken in Ireland. That guy was staring at Patrick as if he wanted to kill him. I just wondered . . .'

'I'm not surprised.'

'You know him?'

'I should. That's Seamus Cummings. Older. And God he's got thin, but that's him.'

I forgot about the coffee. 'How do you know him?'

She turned away from the board and got milk from the fridge.

'Sheila?'

'I thought from the way we . . . went about things, we weren't going into our past histories.' She pointed to Lily's photograph.

'This is different.'

She poured milk into the mugs. 'How?'

'I still want to find out who killed Patrick.'

'I thought you'd decided he was trying to kill you.'

'I haven't decided anything.'

She lowered the plunger, waited the required time and poured. 'Mmm, me either. I don't know if I want to go into it.'

It was one of those moments when something, apparently promising, potentially solid, can fracture at a word or a gesture. I was still unsure about Sheila but I didn't want that to happen. My feelings for her and the hope I felt were too strong. I'd blown these moments too often in the past by reacting too quickly. I slowed down, picked up the mug and blew gently on the surface to cool it. She took her mug and did the same, looking past me, back at the photograph.

'It's all right, Sheila,' I said. 'You don't have to tell me.'

She smiled. We were both tired and affected by the emotional pulls and tugs. Some strands of her well-managed hair had come loose and made her look younger, more vulnerable. I wanted badly to touch her and I think she sensed this.

'Cost you a bit to say that, lover, didn't it?'

I shrugged, drank some coffee.

'Tough guy. Our break-up, Paddy's and mine, was a protracted business, with infidelities on both sides and brief reconciliations. One of my affairs—didn't last and I went back to Paddy briefly—was with him. Seamus Cummings.'

15

Sheila told me that the man she knew as Seamus Cummings, known to Angela Warburton as Sean Cassidy, was, or had been, a soldier. She didn't know in what army he'd served—who he'd fought for or against.

'He was sexy,' she said.

Looking at the photograph, I could see the cause of the attraction, especially when he had a bit more flesh on his bones. He looked confident, and that means more to a lot of women than good looks. Certainly more than a full head of hair or the other things that men worry about and put store in. She said Cummings had never met Patrick as far as she knew, but had seen his photograph.

'He went wild when I told him I was dropping him for Paddy.'

'Violent wild?'

'Not to me; more to himself. He did threaten Paddy, but

instead of doing anything he went on a week-long drunk and finished up in jail.'

'This was where?'

'Brisbane. I was buggering around in a crummy little theatre company and Paddy was still in the army but getting ready to leave.'

We'd finished the coffee and were on the sofa. I was sitting; she was lying with her head on my lap. I stroked her hair. We'd got past the point of antagonism or misunderstanding. She saw that I wasn't probing her, just pursuing a line of inquiry.

'Did Patrick have a beard back then? Say, in the photograph this guy, whatever he calls himself, saw? He certainly recognised him at the *céilidh*.'

'It's a lovely word for a piss-up, isn't it? Let me think. Yeah, I think so. They weren't allowed to have beards in the army, but he was on leave. Paddy's beards were sort of reverse deciduous—on in winter, off in summer.'

We were both tired, more than a little drained by the recent events in our separate and combined lives. Our hands moved, independently, to the places we wanted to touch. Tired can be good.

'One last question,' I said. 'What was Cummings doing in Australia?'

'Jesus, you detective, you. He had family here. People who'd emigrated. He said he came out pretty often to look them up. He wouldn't kill Paddy over something that happened that many years ago, surely.'

Sheila was up early, before me. She spent a lot of time in the bathroom and then on her mobile phone. She skipped breakfast and took off in a hurry. I'd found recently that I needed something in my stomach for the heart medications to lie comfortably, so I sat down to two poached eggs and coffee with my notebook. I drew a firm line through Sheila's name, cancelling her as a suspect. It wasn't just the feelings I had for her. She'd scarcely mentioned her claim on Patrick's estate and was clearly more excited by her acting prospects than anything else, including, I suspected, our relationship. I was sure she wasn't acting now. If she was, she was better than Meryl Streep.

Men don't commit murder over failed love affairs twenty years in the past. I was down to two possibilities—Frank Szabo, or someone connected with Patrick's smuggling activities. The latter seemed more likely but I was unsure how to go about investigating it and, anyway, that would be what the police were concentrating on. I logged on and brought up the Western Warriors website. 'Up Hawkesbury way' translated into a property on the river above Wisemans Ferry.

The web entry gave details of the property and fairly precise directions to it. A photograph of what was called 'The Compound' showed a high cyclone fence with a reception booth. There were telephone and fax numbers for the Commander and the Personnel Officer. Didn't look like a place where you just dropped in.

The WW, as it was styled, described itself as 'dedicated to masculinity, courage, resourcefulness and survival'. The activities included physical training, orienteering, rafting, scuba diving, unarmed combat and war games. It sounded like one of the 'Iron John' outfits popular in the nineties in the US. They spouted right-wing political agendas, of course, but were basically harmless—run by fantasists catering to the insecurities of other fantasists. I'd read that these organisations generally morphed into mechanisms for extracting money from those who signed up. Some switched focus and became wacko cults. It was hard to see Szabo playing those games, but Marvis Marshall had hinted at something more serious with his mention of soldiers of fortune and ordnance. And there was that reference on the website to war games.

Hank called in, checked my landline and gave it the all-clear. He spent some time with the computer and told me he'd installed firewall protection for my emails—whatever that meant. He used the upstairs bathroom and came down sniffing ostentatiously.

'You've got a lady friend, or you're turning weird on us.'

'Mind your own business.'

'Megan'll be pleased. She said she couldn't see you as a long-term celibate.'

I packed a bag, fuelled the Camry and headed north. I had no particular plan for getting inside the WW stronghold, but you can sometimes talk your way past caretakers, concierges, even armed guards. And I'd been over, under and through cyclone fences before.

It was mid-week on a mild, cloudy day. Traffic on the highway is never light but it wasn't too bad and the car handled well. I played some Kasey Chambers, the Whitlams and Perry Keyes' album, *The Last Ghost Train Home*. It rained and the road grew slippery and the trucks threw up oily spray. I turned the music off and concentrated on my driving, glad to leave the freeway at Hornsby.

The road wriggles up past Galston and through Glenorie and Maroota. Nice country and pretty restful driving so that I could play the music again. Not that I really heard it. I was running possible courses of action through my mind. The toy soldiers, for all their openness, might not welcome me or give me time with one of their number. I could ask about them in the place nearest their property—a hamlet called Battle, which might have inspired their choice of site—and feel my way into the situation.

I resisted the impulse to have a drink in one of the Wisemans Ferry pubs, crossed the river on the cable ferry, and pushed on up a road that degenerated from tarmac to dirt to gravel and clay. The country looked lush after recent rain and the river had a strong flow. The road skirted the edge of the national park as the land rose with every kilometre west. I rounded a bend as the road veered away from the river and Battle came into view—from this distance just a collection of tin roofs with some smoke rising in the cold, still air.

The place consisted of a general store with a petrol bowser attached and a handicrafts shop. The shop was closed and looked as though it only opened at its owner's whim, but the store was open for business. It served as a DVD hire, post office, fast food outlet, bottle shop and pool hall. A gossip and information centre if ever I saw one. I was in cords, boots, a flannel shirt and denim jacket and the car had acquired a coating of mud and dust on the trip. I hadn't shaved that morning and I fancied I didn't look like a city slicker.

A man and a woman were working behind the several counters—both overweight, both talking loudly to the four or five customers needing their services. Loudly, because a TV tuned to a game show was blaring. The patrons divided their attention between the TV and their orders, and they ignored me after a cursory glance. Both shopkeepers were flat out, and I wandered around, inspecting the DVDs, a rack of second-hand paperbacks and the pool set-up: two tables with battered surfaces, the cloth lifting in some spots and worn almost bare in others. It was a fair bet that the cues were warped.

Toasted sandwiches, loaves of bread, litres of milk, beer and cigarettes dispensed, the customers filed out one by one after taking last looks at the screen. I was about to approach the counter to buy a six-pack and ask my question when I heard the scrape of boots on the coir mat at the door. A tall man, heavily bearded and wearing a bush hat, modified military fatigues and a Driza-Bone walked in. He saw me, mock saluted, and pulled off his hat.

'Paddy Malloy,' he said. 'What the hell are you doing here?'

16

I must have gaped and my jaw probably dropped. It took me a beat to recover, but by then he'd grabbed my hand and was shaking it hard. He ran his other hand over his bald skull.

'It's Colin Kennedy. Didn't recognise me without the mop, eh, Paddy? Well, it's been a while and some of us've got more testosterone than others, eh? You're looking great, Paddy. Bit greyer, but fit.'

He was a big bear of a man, wide and thick with shoulders like the old-time blacksmiths. There was a tattoo on the back of his left hand. Not a prison job: a flag and a chevron—army.

'Gidday, Colin. Yeah, it's been a while. How long would you say?'

'I'd have to think. Look, I just have to pick up some mail for the camp and then we can have a beer and a yarn.'

'Right, I'll buy the beer. What's your go these days?'

'Fosters, same as ever. Hang on.'

The woman behind the counter was waving a thick stack of envelopes at him and he went across to collect them. I approached the man scraping grease from the hotplate.

'A six-pack of Fosters, thanks, mate.'

'Col only drinks long necks.'

'Six of 'em, then.'

He opened the fridge, took out the bottles and put them in a plastic bag. Kennedy gave me a thumbs-up and we went outside.

'Clem doesn't mind if we crack a couple out here,' Kennedy said. 'The local copper doesn't mind either if he gets one.'

We sat on the bench on the porch outside the shop. Kennedy found a bottle-opener among the metal objects dangling from his belt and whipped the caps off two bottles. We clinked them and drank.

'You mentioned a camp, Col. Wouldn't be the Western Warriors' place, would it?'

'Sure is. Hey, d'you remember that stoush we had with those poofy sailor boys in Townsville? That was a go, eh?'

I never liked Fosters, too sweet, but I downed a bit and undid the top buttons of my shirt to show the scars from my heart operation.

'Fact is, Col,' I said, 'I had a heart attack a while back and it knocked me around a bit. Fucking eight-hour operation, would you believe? They pulled me through it but I lost a bit along the way. Memory's not that flash. Sorry.'

'Shit, mate, sorry to hear it. You were one of the fittest blokes in the unit. Fittest officer, that's for sure, and you didn't pull rank on us NCOs.'

I grinned. 'Yeah. 'Less I had to.'

'When the word came down from above. Right. Well, we were a wild bunch all right, but that was what we were supposed to be.'

I nodded. 'So what're you doing now?'

He had the level of the bottle well down and some of the ebullience was seeping out of him.

'Ah, got into a bit of strife after I left the army. Wife trouble, grog trouble, money trouble, you know.'

'Tell me about it.'

'I'm in with this Western Warriors mob. Bit of a Mickey Mouse show to be honest, but they like a bloke with experience of the real thing. Hey, you haven't said what you're here for, Paddy.'

I thought. I didn't know how long I could sustain the charade. Colin Kennedy obviously hadn't been reading the newspapers. If there were other former comrades of Patrick at the Western Warriors camp it was better than even money that one of them would know he was dead. But if it got me into the place it was worth the risk.

'I'm trying to catch up with a bloke I want to talk to. I heard he was one of this mob, and I thought I'd come up to take a look.'

He drained his bottle. 'Yeah? Who would that be?'

'Frank Szabo.'

'Frankie? Yeah, he's here. How'd you hear about him, Paddy?'

I tapped the side of my head. 'Like I say, I'm a bit vague about where and when.'

His voice took on a solicitous tone. 'You been inside, Paddy?'

I nodded. 'Berrima. While back.'

'Hard case, Frankie, or was. I reckon he'd be glad to talk to you. How about you follow me up there? I'm in the Land Rover. That yours, the Camry?'

'Hired. How's the road?'

'Okay since we put some work into it. Just take it easy.'

I gave him the bag with the remaining bottles. 'For the mess.'

A battered khaki Land Rover stood a few metres from my car and a couple of others that had arrived while we were talking. I'd noticed it, but hadn't seen the 'WW' painted on the door, half covered in mud, until I got closer. It had a vaguely military look, like Kennedy himself.

He reached the 4WD, tossed the mail inside and put the bottles on the passenger seat. He turned back to me and I tensed, because his manner had changed a little.

'You were always a crafty bastard, Paddy. Thinking of joining up, are you?'

I shrugged. 'Probably past it.'

He brushed the side of his nose in the old soldier's gesture. 'We'll see. Stay back a bit and steer round the puddles.'

After a few kilometres the road deteriorated and Kennedy's advice about staying back made sense. Then the surface improved with gravel filling in the potholes and a slight camber on the bends. The bush was thick on both sides as the road sloped up and the air got colder. I had the window down to enjoy the smells and the sounds. A little bit of country air, however cold, does you good. Kennedy speeded up on the better surface; we rounded a bend and the camp came into view.

We crossed a narrow, shallow creek on a concrete ford and then a cattle grid in front of a high gate in a high cyclone fence. Electronic. After a brief pause, the gate swung open; the booth I'd seen in the web photo looked less formidable in reality and was unoccupied. We entered what once must have been a farm of some kind: a few hectares of cleared, flattish land, with a scattering of buildings—an old timber house, a demountable that looked like a schoolroom and two Nissen huts flanking a bituminised square with a flagpole in the middle. Kennedy swung the Land Rover around to where another bitumen strip was marked out as a parking bay. I followed him, stopping beside a canopied truck that looked even more military than the 4WD.

I had the .38 in the shoulder holster but had made sure

the flannie hung loose over it and that the denim jacket didn't promote a bulge. I got out of the car and joined Kennedy as he walked towards the house.

'I'm gonna deliver the mail, check in with the CO and then we'll hunt up Frankie. Out with a skirmish group at this time, I reckon.'

'How many people here, Col?'

'You know better than that, Paddy. Operational information.'

We were close to the house and I saw a man coming through the door. His walk was a self-important strut.

'Who's the pocket Napoleon?'

'Shut your fuckin' trap!' Kennedy snapped as we got closer.

Kennedy presented the mail to the man who stood on the verandah the best part of a metre above him. He needed the extra height—couldn't have topped 155 centimetres. He wore modified military dress like Kennedy, no insignia but the cut of his clothes was superior and his voice had a clipped precision.

'And who is this, Kennedy?'

'Old army mate, sir. Paddy . . . Patrick Malloy. First Lieutenant.'

'Vietnam?'

'Yes, sir.'

He didn't leave the verandah, but he bent and reached down with his hand. 'Peter Foster-Jones, Mr Malloy. Very glad to meet a fellow officer.'

We shook hands and Kennedy explained that I wanted to talk to Francis Szabo. Foster-Jones nodded, lost interest, turned his attention to the mail. 'Carry on, Kennedy.'

I thought, *Francis?* At least there was no saluting.

Kennedy waited until we were out of earshot before he spoke. 'Sorry to snarl at you, Paddy, but that little prick takes all of this very seriously. Or pretends to. I'm not sure. Thing is, it's an easy job, full bed and board and decent pay for us old soldiers. You want to think about it.'

'Okay. Where does the money come from?'

'Who knows? Who cares? Corporations mostly, I reckon. They send executives here for toughening up, leadership training. That shit. Most of 'em've never lifted anything heavier than a golf club.'

We left the cleared area and were walking down a track into the bush. 'Do they benefit from it?'

'Some do, some run screaming back to Mummy.'

Every hundred metres or so, the trees on both sides of the track were marked with splotches of white paint. Kennedy saw me noticing and grinned.

'Orienteering,' he said. 'Some of them've got the sense of direction of a headless chook. They need marks all the way home.'

'What's Szabo's role in all this?'

'You'll see.'

We took a narrow track leading to a creek and Kennedy gestured for me to move slowly and quietly and keep to the trees beside the path. After a minute he stopped and pointed. We were at a high point of the creek bank and, fifty or sixty metres away, I saw a group of men, camouflaged with bits of bush and leaves, wriggling forward on their bellies. They reached the water, hesitated, then kept going, still crawling and keeping their heads above the water. After crossing the creek they leapt up and charged into the bush, shouting and firing.

'Pop guns,' Kennedy said.

'Real water though, and bloody cold.'

'Toughening up.'

Kennedy squatted down and lit a cigarette. 'First of the day,' he said, offering me the packet.

I shook my head.

He gave me a quizzical look. 'You used to be a chain smoker.'

'I quit.'

'How?'

I traced a line down the centre of my chest. 'I had no choice. What're we waiting here for, Col?'

'They'll be along soon, looking like drowned rats.'

About twenty men, carrying weapons I couldn't identify and answering to Kennedy's description, appeared from the bush. They waded across the creek. A few sneezed. They set off along the path in reasonable order. Bringing up the rear was a tall, dark man whose clothes were dry. I'd never laid eyes on him but he was the image of his father: Frank Szabo, son of Soldier.

17

'Hey, Frankie,' Kennedy yelled.

Szabo looked to where we were standing and waved. Kennedy motioned for him to come up. Szabo spoke to a member of the troop and they moved on. Szabo climbed the fairly steep and muddy slope in a few easy strides.

'What's up, Col?'

'Want you to meet an old comrade of mine, Paddy Malloy. We were in 'Nam together.'

Szabo looked at me and at that moment I travelled back mentally twenty years, to when I stared into the yellow, wolfish eyes of Soldier Szabo as he moved in to kill me. The eyes were the same. Szabo drew in a deep breath and balanced himself as if he might go for my throat or my balls. My jacket was open and I knew I could get the pistol quickly if I had to.

Szabo let the breath out slowly. 'No, he's not,' he said. 'He's

Cliff Hardy, the private detective who killed my father.'

'Right,' I said.

Kennedy took a step towards me. 'What the hell's going on?'

I kept my eyes focused on Szabo, who appeared totally relaxed. 'I'm sorry, Kennedy,' I said. 'You gave me an opening and I took it. You may as well know, Patrick Malloy's dead. He was shotgunned in my house. We were cousins, lookalikes, and I'm wondering whether this man killed him instead of me.'

Kennedy unclenched the fist he'd been ready to throw at me and fished out his cigarettes. He lit up. 'I was beginning to wonder about you—not smoking, and you don't move the way Paddy did. Slower.'

'He was a bit younger and he hadn't had a heart attack. We were friends, if that means anything to you.'

Kennedy blew smoke. 'I don't understand any of this. Think I'd better report to the Commander.'

'Don't do that, Col,' Szabo said. 'I'll sort this out and fill you in later. Why don't you catch up with that mob and debrief them. You know the drill.'

Szabo spoke with a quiet authority, clearly respected by Kennedy, who stamped his barely smoked cigarette butt into the mud, shot me a furious look, and strode away.

Szabo waited until Kennedy was back on the path. Then he pointed to my left shoulder. 'You won't need the gun. You shouldn't carry that arm a bit stiff the way you do.'

'I'm out of practice,' I said. 'Convince me.'

'I've bashed people and cut them, kicked them and broken limbs, but I've never killed anyone.'

'You're a known shottie artist.'

'Was.'

'You made threats against me in jail.'

He nodded. 'Some time back. I was a different person then.'

'You bought a shotgun recently.'

'You *have* been busy. I don't know what story you told poor Col. He's not the brightest. I'm guessing you said something about wanting to talk to me and he took you at your word on that.'

'Yes. So?'

He unzipped his jacket. 'Let me show you something.'

'Easy.'

He reached inside his shirt and pulled out a silver cross on a chain.

'I'm the pastor of this flock as well as one of the trainers. I'm a Christian and I wouldn't take revenge on you for killing my father. Revenge is for God. I forgive you, and I hope you forgive yourself.'

'You bought a shotgun.'

'Yeah, I did, and a box of fifty shells and I went out into the bush and fired off every last one. Then I took an angle grinder and cut the gun up into little bits, which I dumped. I purged myself of shotguns and violence. People can change, Hardy.'

'Maybe. I haven't seen it happen all that much.'

'You can believe me or not, as you choose.'

I did believe him. The gleam in his eyes wasn't from the killer instinct his father had displayed; it was the light of redemption, the glow of the saved. I waved my hand at the bush, the creek, the muddy footprints on the path.

'So what's all this, onward Christian soldiers?'

'Your cheap cynicism does you no credit.'

Francis Szabo had picked up some education as well as religion along the way; he had the moral drop on me and I had to acknowledge it.

'I'm sorry,' I said. 'That's the second bloody sorry in a few minutes. Not easy, but you can see where I was coming from when I heard certain things about you.'

'Yes. If you'd inquired a bit more you'd have learned other things and saved yourself a trip.'

We started down towards the path. I slipped and he steadied me. 'I guess I've been talking to the wrong people,' I said.

He didn't say anything until we were back in the centre of the compound. He guided me towards my car.

'I'll have a word at the gate and you can go through.'

'Thanks.'

It was an awkward moment and we both felt it.

I jiggled my keys. 'I don't know what to say.'

'Neither do I,' he said. 'But I'd suggest you take a good look at yourself and the way your life is heading.'

part three

18

I'd run out of candidates for making me the target and my encounter with Szabo hadn't done anything for my confidence or self-esteem. He was right—I should have asked how old Ben Corbett and Marvis Marshall's information was and tried to get a more up-to-date assessment. I was left with the conclusion that the killer had got the man he wanted. I now knew more about Patrick than before, perhaps more than the police knew.

The smart course might be to turn that information over to the police. Then again, that might not be so smart. They might think I was trying to deal myself out of the drug importation charge. These thoughts ran through my head as I made my chastened way back to Sydney. It was the sort of stalemate I'd reached many times before. In the early days I made the mistake of talking it over with Cyn.

'Stop beating your head against a brick wall,' she said.

'Drop it. Move on.'

I never did, and wouldn't now. I still had my conduit to the workings of the police service—Frank Parker, who'd retired as an Assistant Commissioner but was still on their books as an adviser and consultant. I'd overworked and strained the relationship when I was a busy PEA, but I'd also done him some good turns along the way (quite apart from introducing him to his wife), and we'd both mellowed in recent times. I thought I could count on Frank to at least tell me how the police inquiry was progressing. I could take my cue from that.

The first thing I did was to return the pistol and ammunition to Ben Corbett. He'd sell it to someone else before you could turn around, but that wasn't my problem. If a criminal wants a gun he'll get one, and no law will stop him, or her. Corbett examined the weapon carefully.

'Not fired.'

'Never sniffed the air.'

'Two hundred back.'

'That's a bit light on, even for you.'

'Because I'm charging you for some information you'll be interested in.'

'Go on.'

He handed me the two notes. 'Deal?'

'Why not?'

'I've got this mate who's a fuckin' ballistics expert. He runs this little show and the cops put work his way. What's it called, that?'

'Outsourcing.'

'Right. Anyway, we chew the fat and he tells me about examining these shotgun pellets taken from a bloke killed in Glebe recently. I read the papers. That'd be the hit that went down at your place, right?'

I nodded.

'I'm thinking you wanted the .38 to go after the guy who did the job but you didn't find him. So this information might be worth something to you.'

'Good thinking, Ben.'

'Not as dumb as what you thought, eh? He says the pellets were self-loaded. That's unusual, but what's weirder is that they were treated with some kind of poison. Get the idea? You hit some fucker at the end of the range and don't kill him, but the poison gets him anyway. Cute, eh?'

'Yes. What else? I can see you're dying to tell me.'

'My mate reckons there's a particular mob that went in for this trick—blokes who fought in them African wars a while back. Not army, what're they called?'

'Mercenaries.'

'Good money, they say. Tax free. Should have had a go at it myself.'

'You have to kill women and children and burn villages.'

'Whoopee!'

I'd switched off my mobile for the trip north. I turned it on when I got home and there was a message from Sheila to say that she'd visit that evening if I confirmed. I did. I wanted to see her, not only for the shared pleasure, but because I wanted to get every scrap of information she had about Patrick. Someone out there hated him enough to make absolutely sure of killing him and the reason had to lie somewhere in his past. It was going to be a tricky balancing act—loving and interrogating—and I rehearsed some of the questions I'd put as I cleaned myself up.

I went out for wine and bread and cheese and enjoyed the feeling of not having to watch my back. I could return the Camry, but I'd still keep my communications secure from the police, at least until I'd spoken to Frank.

Sheila arrived about 10 pm. I hadn't eaten since breakfast and neither had she, so, after the usual enthusiastic preliminaries, we got stuck into the food and the wine.

I decided to start by telling her about the parcel from London and the steroids and how I was facing a charge of importing them.

She put down her glass. 'You didn't tell me about a parcel coming from London.'

'That was when I didn't know what you were up to.'

'Now you do?'

'I hope so.'

'Why are you telling me this now?'

'Because I'm sure now Patrick was the target, not me, and

I still want to find out who killed him. I need to know every scrap of information about him.'

'Why are you so sure?'

I told her about the trip north and the result. How I came back with my tail between my legs. Then I told her about the poisoned shot pellets. She finished her wine and held out her glass for more. She'd had one go at the bread and cheese compared with my three or four. More than most, Sheila was someone who could discipline herself.

'Are you in serious trouble over the steroids?'

'Hard to say. Depends on the cops. I'm hoping to get a line on their attitude to me and their investigation of Patrick's murder. I'm not in good standing with the police, but I've got one friend with contacts.'

'You must wish Paddy'd never turned up.'

I looked at her. She was tired with lines showing around her eyes and mouth under her fresh makeup. Her hair was caught in some kind of bun with a few strands coming loose. She was wearing her suit again with a blouse not as crisp as before. I felt protective and lustful—a potent combination. I pushed the plates aside, reached for her and pulled her close.

'If I hadn't met him, I wouldn't have met you.'

That ended the eating and drinking and the discussion. We went upstairs.

Sheila didn't rush away in the morning as she had before. We took our time getting up, showering, dressing and having breakfast. She saw me taking my meds and grimacing at the sweet taste of the aspirin.

'Rest of your life, eh?'

'However long that may be.'

'I'd back you in for eighty, Cliff.'

She said she didn't have any meetings to do with the film for a few days, but that she was reading the script and doing research on the sort of woman her character was—the criminal matriarch.

'A few of them about,' she said. 'You could be useful here. Ever run into one of them?'

'Thankfully no. I remember what Frank Parker, the cop friend I mentioned, said when he had dealings with Kitty "Cat Woman" Saunders.'

'I've read about her. She was a piece of work. Hang on, I'll jot this down.'

'He said, "If you ever meet one of these women run a mile, because she'll do you harm".'

She scribbled in a tiny notebook. 'That's good. I'd like to meet this guy.'

'You will. Can you answer a few more questions about Patrick?'

She sighed. 'I guess so. Will he always be in the room?'

'No. That's partly why I'm doing this, I realise. I want to kind of exorcise him. He was in Vietnam, right? D'you think he ever suffered the post traumatic stuff—the nightmares, the jumping at shadows . . .'

She took a long time to answer and I saw that the memories were painful.

'Sorry,' I said, 'if it's too hard don't—'

'It's okay. I got over it, just a bit hard to go back to all the pain now that things are looking up and we're . . . Well, I got pregnant and Paddy went off his head. He said he'd walked through clouds of agent orange and any child of his would be lucky to be born with only one head . . .'

She burst into tears and I comforted her as best I could. After some sniffing and nose-blowing she recovered. 'He made me have an abortion, and he went straight out and had a vasectomy. Is that the sort of thing you mean?'

I wanted to ask about his dealings with the mercenary brigade, whatever it was, but I'd pushed her far enough. She went to the bathroom and repaired her makeup while I tidied away the breakfast things thinking that I was hitting more faults than aces lately. I reproached myself—sports metaphors are too easy. I was getting involved with this woman and wounding her in the process. She came back, smelling of too much perfume. We kissed and she left. A shaky parting.

I returned the Camry, collected the Falcon and drove to Paddington to see Frank. The drive took longer than it should have because the Pope was in town for a few days with a couple of hundred thousand of his admirers and the traffic patterns had been changed to make them even more unfriendly than they already were. I'd rung and Frank was expecting me, meaning he had a couple of bottles of Heineken to hand.

We sat by the pool in a patch of sunshine.

'His Holiness brought good weather,' Frank said as he lifted the caps.

'He did; hope he leaves it behind him when he goes.'

'I can read you like a book, Cliff. Who is she?'

'What do you mean?'

'You get a certain look when you're on with someone.'

'Shit, not smug and self-satisfied I hope.'

'No. Sort of pleased and grateful.'

'That'd be right.'

The beer was going down well. I filled Frank in on all the developments, including my relationship with Sheila, but with a certain amount of editing—about the .38 for example. There was still enough of the straight-as-a-die cop about him for that information to have pissed him off. When I told him about the poisoned pellets, without mentioning the extra bit of knowledge I had on that, he nearly choked on his beer.

'How the hell do you know that?'

'Outsourcing is another word for leaking.'

'You're right. So Frankie Szabo's born again. D'you believe that?'

'I believe it for now. He didn't kill Patrick. Whether it'll hold when the born-again thrill wears off's another question. They find it hard to hack the normal.'

'Like you. You should leave this alone, Cliff. There's some good people working on it.'

I shook my head. 'Time's passing. You know how it is; the longer it takes the harder it gets. I need to know if they're making any progress. I need to know how hard they're trying. They've got Patrick pegged as a steroids importer. That lowers their interest. Serves him right.'

'It's you facing that charge.'

'That's bullshit. You know it and they must know it.'

'I dunno. You liked this bloke. You might have done him a favour.'

'I didn't like him *that* much. Just tell me this, is that the line they're working on—the steroids?'

He shrugged. 'As far as I know. If you've got another line, Cliff, you should talk to them. You've got no standing, no protection.'

'When did I ever have?'

'You had more than you knew. One tip. I know how you work; you're not a complete cowboy. Ian Welsh's a good man. If you get in too deep contact him.'

'Will you be talking to him?'

'All depends. It's a strange world we live in.'

'You're right,' I said. 'Three hundred thousand people at Randwick racecourse, and not a horse in sight.'

19

They've cracked down on steroids in sport. About body-building, I wasn't sure, but my feeling was there was less interest generally in that these days than in the past. Maybe because Arnie had gone political and Sly and Rocky and Rambo were winding down. But I knew of one area of activity where they were still used and where I had contacts.

I'd worked a few times as a bodyguard for film and television actors and in that role I'd naturally fallen into conversation with stuntmen like Ben Corbett. Corbett was what was known in the film and television world as a 'wheelie', specialising in motorised stunts, but there were others, particularly 'swingers', who performed athletic jumping, falling, hanging—essentially gymnastic—illusions. They had to be strong and quick and they regularly injured themselves but needed to keep working because they weren't well paid.

They used steroids to build strength but, more importantly, to recover from strains, pulls, dislocations. These people, mostly men but including a few women, paid very high insurance premiums and the movie production companies did the same to safeguard themselves against lawsuits in the event of accidents. The stunters had to pass frequent medical tests and it was a fair bet that they'd try to mask their use of steroids. Patrick's pills could look attractive in that context.

Toby Fairweather had done some of the stunts for one of the actors I'd bodyguarded in a film that involved a lot of climbing, swinging, jumping and diving. I'd been impressed by the careful way he'd gone about setting everything up to minimise the risks. He was a disciplined guy, didn't drink when working, and was a fitness fanatic. But he admitted that his body had taken a battering over the years and that he used steroids to keep going. I thought he'd know how the market stood, how high the stakes were.

When Toby's not stunting or working out in the gym, he conducts early morning and late afternoon classes in Chinese fighting sticks, conducted in Camperdown Park. Good little earner, low overhead. I threaded through the traffic and the singing, dancing pilgrims and got there when a class was in full swing. There were four pupils, two men and two women, and Toby was putting them through their paces, switching them from one-on-one combat to a sort of all-in melee and then cutting one out and taking that one on himself. The pupils were young, in their late teens and early twenties; two Asian, two not. Toby is forty plus but was clearly faster and more deft than any of them, although they all showed promise.

I sat on a seat and watched as the light faded. The clatter of the sticks and the grunts and occasional screeches attracted a few bystanders. When the session finished, some of the watchers clapped before drifting away. Toby bowed, all style. He collected the sticks, spoke briefly to the youngsters, picked up his bag and sauntered over to where I was sitting.

'Hi, Cliff. Great exercise and very calming. You should try it.'

'Gidday, Toby. I've been hit on the head too many times already, thanks, and I'm calm enough.'

He sat and tied the sticks into a bundle with a length of cord and put them into his long bag—the kind cricketers use. 'You're never calm,' he said. 'You don't have a calm aura.'

'I do my best. I need some information, Toby. Do you want to go somewhere up King Street for herbal tea?'

He laughed. 'Love to take the piss, don't you? No, I'm happy here. I've got a stunt rehearsal to go to soon. What's up?'

I told Toby as much as he needed to know about Patrick's steroids. He listened intently while squeezing a rubber ball in each of his hands as a wrist strengthening exercise. I suppose you need strong wrists when hanging from bridges and swinging on ropes across rivers.

'Built-in masking agent, you reckon,' he said. 'Those things would be worth a lot of money. Didn't happen to hang on to a handful, did you?'

'Who'd want them, apart from would-be suicides like you? Athletes? Footballers?'

He shook his head. 'Not worth it, but lots of people—truckies with injuries and getting too old for the game; tuna fishermen, same thing; police rescue boys and girls; mountaineers, rock climbers, cavers—you name it.'

I thought about Patrick's remark: *I have a thought or two.* 'Is there enough money in it for someone to get killed for doing the wrong thing?'

'You mean ripping off a consignment?'

'Something like that, or horning in on an established market.'

'I don't think it's organised enough for that. More a matter of people seeing an opportunity and grabbing it, but I could ask around. Who's got the stuff we're talking about now?'

'Dunno. Police or Customs.'

'It'll filter through, then, at least some of it. I'll keep an eye out.'

I thanked him and had got up to leave when he pushed me down and pointed to the suture scar just showing above the top button of my shirt.

'That what I think it is?'

I nodded. 'Bypass.'

'What did I tell you when I saw you tucking into steak and chips on that movie set?'

'The catering was too flash to resist.'

'Things've changed. It's pies and sausage rolls now, if you're

164

lucky. Doesn't bother me of course. Well, see you, Cliff. Glad you're still in the land of the living, even though you don't deserve to be.'

Toby is a vegetarian. He loped away and I watched him disappear into the gathering gloom. I was hearing that sort of news too much lately from people in various professions—restricted services, belt tightening.

As I got up and stretched, joints cracking, two men came slouching towards me. One was about my height and build, the other shorter and wider. They were both young and carrying stubbies.

'Hey, mate, got a spare smoke?' the taller one said.

'No, sorry.'

Shorty said, 'Got a light?'

'Why would I have a light if I haven't got a cigarette?'

'You're a smartarse,' Shorty said.

'And you're a nuisance. Go away.'

The taller one said, 'I bet he's got a wallet.'

'Go away before you get hurt.'

He reached out and grabbed the lapel of my jacket. Bad move. Two free hands will usually beat none. I hit him hard over the heart. He dropped to his knees and vomited. The other man swung at my head with his bottle. Another mistake—too small a target and a head can duck. Go for the body first. I gave him a right rip to the ribs and when he sagged I lifted my knee and caught him under the chin. He collapsed and his bottle hit the graffiti-covered brick wall and smashed.

I bent down, lifted him, and propped him against the wall under a peace sign. 'Look after your mate. He's not feeling well.'

I walked away. The confrontation had taken a matter of seconds and the few other people in the park were too far away to see what happened.

I drove home. Sheila's VW was parked across from my house. She got out as I arrived; we embraced in the middle of the street, and she stepped back sniffing.

'What?' I said.

'Funny smell.'

We went into the house and when we were under the light she pointed to my pants below the knee. 'Ugh, you've got chuck all over you.'

I'd been massaging a bruised knuckle. She noticed. She put down her bag with a thump. 'What happened, Cliff?'

'Couple of wannabe muggers.'

'Did they hurt you? No, you hurt them, didn't you?'

'They were young and inexperienced and probably drunk. It's nothing to be proud of. Let me get cleaned up. Did I say I was glad to see you?'

'No, but you will be. I've pulled myself together and I'm ready to tell you everything I can about Paddy and to show you a few things as well.'

I changed my clothes and we sent out for Vietnamese

food. Sheila was animated, almost hectic, high on the prospect of the film and fascinated by the character she was playing. Her research had gone well and reports from the producer, getting the money together, and the director, scouting locations, were good. She drank a few glasses of wine and hoed into the fish and vegetables but scarcely touched the rice. I'd never mastered chopsticks; Sheila was adept. She tried to instruct me as others had done but I was hopeless. The sore hand didn't help.

'You must really have belted him,' she said. 'You were a boxer like Paddy, weren't you?'

I was glad we'd reached the subject. 'He was a pro, I was an amateur.'

'Mr Modest.' She got up, fetched her bag and sat on the couch. 'Come over here.'

I drained my glass and went. The extra weight in her bag turned out to be a hefty photograph album. She opened it over our close-together knees. Sheila was a keen photographer and a good one. She'd kept an extensive photographic record of her tortured relationship and marriage to Patrick Malloy from the days of their meeting at a party to the final split—a shot of Patrick storming off towards his car. Good times and bad times; smiles and tears; presents and the aftermath of rows—smashed glasses, scattered books, broken furniture.

'You can see how it was,' she said. 'We'd break up, go off with someone else and get back together again. Look, here's Seamus Cummings and here's one of the women Paddy was fucking, one of many. I took that without her knowing, jealous as hell.'

The photographs were more or less in chronological order and carried captions: 'Paddy beating me at pool', 'Our wedding', 'Us at Kakadu', etc.

Sheila leaned towards me. 'I bet you looked exactly like him at the same age. What d'you think?'

'Pretty much. Just a bit more handsome.'

'Huh. Just as cocksure, if you know what I mean.'

There were several photos of Patrick in military uniform looking pleased with himself, and one near the end of the collection of him in what looked like a bushman's outfit. Not exactly fatigues, more the movie version of fatigues. He'd put on weight and grown a bristly moustache and didn't look much like me at all.

'What's this?' I said. 'I never looked like that.'

'That's his African outfit.'

'I thought you'd broken up permanently by then.'

'We had, but he turned up. He was always turning up out of the blue and causing trouble.'

'What was the name of that group? Did he ever tell you? He shouldn't have, but since he was showing off . . .'

'He was drunk and unhappy. He didn't care what he said. He did mention a name, but I forget—something Greek. Hercules, Parthenon . . .'

'Well, he never made it to Africa.'

'Why d'you say that?'

'He told me he quit the mercenary mob in England when he learned what they were headed for. Deserted, he said.'

'That's not true. He went to Africa, all right. Look.'

She pulled a postcard from its plastic sleeve and handed it to me. It showed a bush village with characteristic African flat-top trees in the background. The message read: 'Shillelagh, glad you're not here. Love, Paddy.' The card was postmarked Luanda, Republic of Angola.

20

Sheila went off to Melbourne to do more research for her part, this time to talk to people with information about the female role in the gang wars. She said a member of the production team was going with her, a karate expert.

'He'd better be an expert in a bit more than that.'

'Like what?'

'Australian football, dining in Carlton, catching trams, coats and scarves . . .'

'I gather you don't like Melbourne.'

'Nothing good ever happened to me there. You'll be right. Have fun—not too much.'

'What're you going to do?'

'The usual. Talk to people who know things I need to know.'

A web search for Australian mercenary soldiers turned up only one useful item—a book entitled *Diggers for Hire* by John

Casey, published by Partisan Press in 2007. Thanks to the software loaded by Lily and transferred to my new computer, I had Sydney University's Fisher Library catalogue online and found that the book was in the research section. I walked to the university past all the restoration and enhancement work being done on Glebe Point Road to run into major work going on inside the campus. Holes in the ground, cranes, noise—not exactly the dreaming spires. I threaded my way through detours and diversions to the library, made an inquiry and was directed to the right section. A ticket that allows you to borrow costs a fortune, but there's nothing to stop you reading inside the place. The book was mercifully slim and I sat down with it and a notebook. I haven't had much to do with university libraries since my less than successful student days when I was supposed to be studying law but was more interested in other things.

John Casey was a professor at Macquarie University, a former soldier and no stylist. The introduction nearly put me to sleep in the musty, air-conditioned atmosphere and I was relieved to see that the book had an index. I worked through it looking for anything Greek, and the only likely reference was to something called the Olympic Corps. The reference was limited to one paragraph:

The Olympic Corps is a shadowy organisation that may indeed be no more than a rumour. It has been mentioned by former soldiers, but no actual member has ever been identified. All

*information about it is, as far as my researches show, hearsay.
One person has heard something about it from another and
that information is elaborated on and extended by a further
account, which turns out to have no more solid foundation.
Lurid stories are told of African, Pacific and Caribbean
adventures having more the ring of airport fiction than reality.
Official sources, with detailed information about such bodies as
Sandline, are silent about the Olympic Corps, sometimes called
the Corps Olympic. It may be a military myth.*

In a footnote, the author said that FOI approaches to the
Department of Defence and the Attorney-General's Department had met with no reply at the time of the book going
to press. I emailed the professor that I had some information
about the Olympic Corps and would like to meet him to
discuss it. I was about to log off when the chime told me I
had a message. Casey must have been at the computer when
my message arrived because he'd replied immediately, giving
me his phone number and asking me to contact him a.s.a.p.

I did.

'Jack Casey.'

'It's Cliff Hardy, professor.'

'Good. Have you got a secure line?'

'I believe so, yes.'

'Mine is, as far as I know, but let's keep it short. Where
and when can we meet?'

He lived in Balmain and we fixed on a Darling Street pub

at 3 pm. This felt like progress of some kind. I photocopied the passage in Casey's book, left the library and walked home. When I got there a car was parked outside my house and a uniformed police officer stepped out of it and approached me.

'Mr Hardy?'

We'd seen each other at the Glebe station. 'You know it is.'

He opened the rear door of the car. 'Please accompany me to the station.'

'Why?'

'Just get in.'

I unshipped my mobile and stepped back. 'Not until I know why.'

'Under the terms of your bail you're required to report—'

'Jesus Christ, I forgot.'

They made me wait at the station while they filled in forms, made phone calls, twiddled their thumbs. Then they read me the riot act, warning me that another violation could bring the cancellation of my bail, arrest and the loss of part of my bond. I gritted my teeth and took it. When they finally let me go there was barely time to get to Balmain to meet the professor. I was certainly ready for a drink.

Prof Casey was no tweedy bookworm. I'd given him my description over the phone. The man who jumped to his feet and waved a copy of his book at me was late forties, of medium height, solidly built with thick hair and a bushy beard—both dark with a lot of grey. He wore jeans, a grey Harvard T-shirt and a black leather jacket. There was a carafe of red wine on his table with two glasses. Looked like he'd already made a solid start.

'Mr Hardy, I'm Jack Casey.'

'Cliff,' I said. We shook hands.

'I'm on the red. You want something else?'

'Red's fine.'

We sat down and he poured. His copy of *Diggers for Hire* had seen a lot of work: the spine was broken and the corners of pages had been turned down and bits of paper were sticking up. I took out my photocopied page with the footnote highlighted. I took a big slug of the wine.

'You said you had information about Olympic Corps.'

'That's right.' I pointed to the highlighting. 'I'm hoping you've had more luck with this.'

He put on reading glasses and peered. 'I get it. We're swapping, are we? What's your profession, Cliff?'

'I *was* a private detective, now . . .'

'Ah, yes, it comes back to me. You got the flick.'

'That's right. Now I'm investigating the death of someone I *think* may have belonged to this mercenary mob.'

'Why?'

'He was my cousin and it happened in my house.'

He went up in my estimation by not saying he was sorry.

Why should he be? He took a swallow of wine and examined me closely. 'Convince me you're not a spook of some kind.'

I laughed. 'They wouldn't have me, and I wouldn't have a bar of them. I've met a few in my time, a couple were all right, but most of 'em couldn't tell their arses from their elbows. They might've got better, of course.'

He shook his head. 'They haven't—worse if anything in this paranoid climate, which I hope is cooling.'

It was a standoff. I might have asked the same question as him. Universities have always harboured intelligence people, but Casey didn't strike me as a candidate. I took Sheila's photograph of Patrick in Africa from my pocket and the postcard.

'This is the man I'm talking about, and this is a postcard he sent from a certain place. I'll tell you more if you reciprocate.'

He studied the photo, took off his glasses, wiped them on a ragged tissue, and looked closely again. 'Fuck me,' he said. 'This could really be something. See those inverted chevrons? I've seen photos of mercenaries wearing those in . . .'

'Angola. That's where P . . . he sent a postcard from.'

'Right. Who is this guy?'

I took the photo back. 'Whoa. Give and take. Tell me why you asked me if my line was secure, and what's all that about spooks? And I want to hear about the FOI request.'

'Then you'll tell me who he is?'

'Was. I might, under certain conditions.'

'That's a hard bargain.'

I finished off the red and poured another glass, 'Take it or leave it.'

He reached down for the backpack under the table and pulled out a sheaf of papers. I'd seen others like them many times before. They were governmental files but these had the identity of the department and practically the whole of their content blacked out. He leafed through the sheets, showing me that barely a sentence or two per page was complete.

'National security,' he said.

'Tell me about the photos of the mercenaries you saw.'

He pointed to the photo in my hand. 'Who?'

'You first.'

'Okay. It was of a bunch of unidentified white mercenaries shackled together and apparently on their way to prison. Or maybe not.'

'Meaning?'

'Both sides did nasty things to each other in that war. I should say *all* sides because there were quite a few. I'm talking about mutilations and beheadings of the living and the dead. Killing prisoners was routine.'

'His name was Patrick Malloy. Someone blew him apart with a shotgun.'

He gulped down some more wine, took a small box from the pocket of his jacket, opened it and sniffed up a pinch of powder. 'Snuff,' he said. 'Only way to use tobacco inside these days.'

'I'm waiting for the sneeze.'

'Doesn't always happen. There's a security angle to all this, obviously. But a shotgun doesn't sound like our lot.'

'I wouldn't be too sure,' I said. 'There's always out-sourcing.'

21

It was murky—maybe right up Casey's street but not mine. I'd never cultivated contacts in what journalists called the intelligence community because, as I'd told him, I had little respect for the species. What did the CIA predict about the fall of the Berlin Wall, the break-up of the Soviet Union, the fall of the Shah, Marcos and Soeharto? Nothing, and I doubted that their Australian counterparts were any better informed. I told Casey all I could about Patrick and he was encouraged to dig deeper into the photographs he now thought could be of the Olympic Corps, undertaking to keep me informed. He agreed not to publish anything about Patrick until after I'd either found his killer or given up.

The rough red had given me a headache. I bought some painkillers and walked down Darling Street to the water to allow them to work and me to think. Balmain had changed since I arrived in the inner west. It was no longer the habitat of waterside workers, tradesmen, boxers, footballers and bohemians. Gentrified to the max, it had been renovated, speed-bumped, mosaic-paved and priced into a middle-class haven. 4WDs lined the narrow streets and cute little lofts pushed up through the roofs to gain the all-important, property-enhancing water glimpse.

But the water itself was still the same, despite the demise of slips and the surfeit of yachts, and was still balm for the troubled mind. I watched a ferry unload the day's commuters and take on the evening's city-bound fun seekers, and looked across to where lights were marking out the bridges and buildings and felt glad to be part of it, problems and all.

With Sheila away and no obvious avenues to follow, I spent a good part of the next morning in the gym trying to make up for days missed. Wes Scott, the owner and a friend, watched me on the treadmill and shook his head when I stepped off, wringing wet.

'Man, I don't want you dying in my gym.'

Wes is West Indian, a former all-round sportsman and philosopher of the human condition. When he sees someone bludging he's gently critical, when he sees someone overdoing it he's harsh.

'Can't think of a better place to die,' I said. 'Lay me down easy on a padded bench and cover me with a sweaty towel.'

'Take it easy, Cliff. You're in good shape for a man your

age who's been split up the middle. What're you trying to prove?'

I picked up a set of weights. 'Wes, I'm just filling in time waiting for a brilliant idea to strike me. I thought the endorphins might help.'

'Never known it to happen. My best ideas come to me in my sleep.'

'Tried that, didn't work.'

'Depends who you're sleeping with. Ah, sorry, man, I forgot about Lily and . . .'

'It's all right,' I said. 'And would you believe, an idea just came to me.'

He moved smoothly the way a few 190 plus centimetre, one hundred plus kilo men can, and took the weights from me. He handed me a lighter set. 'Don't burn it away. We're only given so many.'

It was Frank's idea, really, to contact Ian Welsh and see what line the police were taking on Patrick's case and what progress they'd made. Depending on what I was told, I'd consider whether to let them know about the mercenary angle. I phoned Welsh from the street.

'Ian Welsh.'

'It's Cliff Hardy, Chief Inspector.'

'Yes.'

'I wonder if we could have a talk.'

'About what? Certainly not the charges pending against you.'

'No, your investigation of Patrick Malloy's murder.'

There was a long pause, so long I thought the line might have dropped out. Then I heard him clear his throat and his voice took on a less assertive tone. 'I suppose we could do that. I suggest we meet.'

That was a surprise. 'When?'

'Where are you now?'

'Outside a gym in Norton Street, Leichhardt.'

'Isn't there a park around there?'

'There is.'

'I could meet you there in half an hour.'

Why not in your office? I thought. Senior police officers don't usually meet civilians in suburban parks. But I agreed. I walked to the park and scouted it thoroughly for vantage points and escape routes. Frank had said Welsh could be trusted, but maybe Frank wasn't up to date. I decided to wait at a spot where I could see what cars arrived around the perimeter and from where I could slip away into a lane if I didn't like the look of things. Drunken muggers in parks are one thing; rogue cops are quite another. It was a nervous wait.

I needn't have worried. Right on time, a car pulled up on the other side of Norton Street and Welsh got out. He waited for the traffic to clear and crossed quickly. No other cars arriving. No suspicious strollers or joggers. Welsh was underdressed for the cold day. He buttoned his suit coat and hunched his shoulders as he hurried up the path. I was sitting on a bench by a hedge that gave me a little protection from the wind. His hair, which I remembered as being carefully arranged to conceal its thinness, was wispy and flying, revealing his pink skull.

He nodded and sat on the bench.

'Look,' I said, 'I know I'm a bit of a pariah these days, but . . .'

'It's not that. I suppose you've ignored my advice and have gone on looking into this matter.'

'I told you I would.'

'You did, and if things were . . . normal, I'd either tear strips off you or try to get you to tell me what you've found out.'

'I was ready for both of those. So things aren't normal?'

He sighed and rubbed his hands together to warm them. It's hard to put your hands in the pockets of a suit coat. Mine were tucked away cosily in the deep pockets of my zipped-up leather jacket.

'The investigation into your cousin's death has been discontinued. I wouldn't be at all surprised if those charges against you are dropped.'

'Why?'

I could see that he was bursting to tell me and hated the fact that he couldn't. Frank was right; this was a decent man trying to do a decent job with malign forces arrayed against him. I gave him the out.

'The spooks've closed you down and threatened you.'

He stood shivering in the wind and patting uselessly at his disarranged hair. 'I didn't say that, and this meeting never took place.'

22

Two days later Viv Garner rang to tell me, as Welsh had predicted, that the charge of importing the steroids had been dropped.

'Insufficient evidence,' he said. 'You lead a charmed life.'

I didn't have the heart to tell him why. I just thanked him and told him to send me his bill.

'You sound depressed.'

'Frustrated.'

'That's a temporary condition.'

'I hope so.'

The trouble was, I couldn't see any way to alleviate it. I scanned the photo of Patrick into the computer and sent it to Jack Casey. He rang to thank me but said he hadn't turned up anything new except that Patrick wasn't one of the men in the photograph of the shackled mercenaries. I went to the gym, went out to dinner with Megan and Hank and drank too much. I had two phone calls from Sheila, which helped a little.

Then I got an email from Angela Warburton in London.

Dear Cliff

You might think I'm pursuing you and maybe I am. Anyway, I'm coming back home soon. Had enough of this country with its class consciousness and all that. Looks like I've got a job with a documentary film-maker who's got six projects lined up and funded. This came about because I had another crack at the photo essay on the Travellers and it turned out well. Got a bit of attention. Sean Cassidy wasn't around. You might be interested to learn that he left for Australia a day or so after you two were here. According to old Paddy he was going to look up members of his family and attend some kind of get-together of descendants of Travellers in Kangaroo Valley this month. Wish I could be there and do a follow-up on my Irish piece, but I won't be back till next month. I'll look you up. Maybe we could go for a surf when the weather warms.

Ciao,

Angie

I read that and sat back. Sean Cassidy, aka Seamus Cummings, who'd had an affair with Sheila, looked daggers at Patrick and had been a soldier of some kind. In Australia by the time Patrick and I got back. Could it be? I emailed the shot of him I'd taken at the *céilidh* to Casey asking, without giving him the name, if Cassidy/Cummings showed up in the photograph of the mercenaries in Angola.

He sounded excited when he rang me.

'It could be, could be. He's a lot thinner, but those guys were thin and super fit. Funny thing is, it could be one of two in the group who look almost identical.'

'What're the chances, on a scale of ten?'

'I'd say eight. Who is he?'

'Have you got a database of known mercenaries from Australia?'

'Yes.'

'Can I see it?'

'It's taken years to compile . . .'

'This man is in Australia.'

'Jesus, if I could talk to him.'

I'd phoned the Kangaroo Valley Tourist Association about the date of its Travellers meeting. 'I know where he's going to be soon. I'm not expecting you to email or fax the bloody thing. Let me have a look at the database on your computer. Be very interesting if there's a match.'

'What if there's not?'

'I'd still want to meet him.'

'You'd put me in touch with him?'

Why not? I thought. 'Yes, although it could be risky. You realise what you could be letting yourself in for?'

'This could be the man who killed your cousin.'

'Right.'

'Hardy, I'm ex-SAS myself and I've been working on this stuff for a long time. I've met some very hard cases in dodgy places.'

Not as hard as this, if he's the man, I thought, but I agreed that we'd go together.

'It'd take a day or two. Can you get the time off?'

'I'd fucking *take* it!'

He gave me his address in Balmain and I arranged to be there that evening.

Jack Casey had everything a successful academic looks for—a sandstone terrace with a water view, a good-looking wife, two kids—a boy and a girl—and a book-lined study. Briskly, he introduced me to his wife and the children before taking me off to the study with a bottle of red wine and two glasses. Evidently the inside smoking ban extended to the house, because the room didn't smell of tobacco and his snuff box was on a shelf above the computer. He poured two glasses of Merlot and switched on the computer.

I studied the room as the computer booted up. No framed degrees, no military insignia. There was a photograph of his wife and another of the two kids and one of a football team. A younger, still bearded version of Casey was sitting in the middle row holding a football. The captain, apparently. I browsed the bookshelves—orderly, but not obsessively so. A low shelf held a few copies of *Diggers for Hire* and multiples of two other titles by Casey—*The Great Lie* and *After Vietnam*. I pulled a copy of the Vietnam title out and turned around when I heard the keys being tapped.

'You're too young for Vietnam,' I said.

'Gulf one. You?'

'Earlier. What've you got there?'

'A list of all the Australian mercenaries I've been able to trace post the Korean War. This is where I learn the name of your bloke, unless I'm supposed to leave the room.'

I laughed and drank some of the wine. 'I wouldn't abuse your hospitality like that, Jack. Try Sean Cassidy.'

He hit the keys. 'No match.'

'Try Seamus Cummings.'

'That name rings a bell. Here we go. Bingo. Yeah, I remember now—Seamus and Liam Cummings.'

Casey printed out two short dossiers:

Seamus Kelly Cummings, d.o.b. 2.1.56, Galway, Republic of Ireland, emigrated to Australia 1964; Australian Army (Sgt) 1975, discharged 1978; I.R.A. 1980–4; imprisoned 1984–7; rumoured mercenary Namibia 19xx (see interview 12a/765). Whereabouts unknown.

Liam Kelly Cummings, d.o.b. 1.10.56, Galway, Republic of Ireland, emigrated to Australia, 1964; Australian CMF 1976–?; rumoured I.R.A. ?—?; rumoured mercenary Namibia 19xx (see interview 12a/765). Whereabouts unknown.

'A couple of boyos, to be sure,' Casey said. 'Practically twins. Has to be them.'

He got the photograph of the captured mercenaries on the screen and blew it up. We studied the faces of the two who resembled my photo of Cassidy/Cummings. Making allowance for weight loss and the different conditions under which the photographs were taken, I was reasonably sure that one of the men was a match.

'Which one?' Casey said.

'Take your pick. What's this interview you've cited?'

'It was with a guy who claimed to be a sort of recruiting agent for an English organisation providing mercenaries for Africa.'

'Claimed to be?'

'That's why I labelled his information as rumour. He seemed to be on the level, but I couldn't get confirmation.'

'What did he say about the photograph?'

'No, that came from another source, not the recruiter. This bloke was a camera freak but pretty solid, I thought. I'm ahead of you—he might be able to throw some light on it. We're still in touch. I could probably see him soon.'

'How soon?'

Casey took a pinch of snuff, didn't sneeze and swigged some more of his very good wine. 'You said you know how to locate this Cummings. When are you going to do that?'

As I'd anticipated, we were back to dealing. Fair enough. I told him about the Travellers meeting and suggested that he

Googled it because his web research skills were better than mine. It didn't take him long to find that 'descendants of the Irish Travelling families now living in Australia were invited to gather at the O'Loughlin farm in Kangaroo Valley on the weekend of 2–3 August to celebrate their heritage'.

'A week off,' Casey said.

'Can you get to your informant before then?'

'I'll try.'

'Tell you what, I've got two bottles of Jamesons we brought back, in case he happens to be Irish.'

'That'd help and he is. How'd you know that?'

'I didn't, but there's nothing but the bloody Irish in this thing. Casey, for God's sake.'

He laughed. 'It's an Anglicisation of something Polish and unpronounceable, but I've been known to trade on it. I'll get busy. Jesus, something solid on Olympic Corps, that'd be a coup.'

'A footnote?'

'An article at the very least, maybe an update of the book, and a poke in the eye for those FOI bastards.'

'Don't get carried away. If he's the man who killed Patrick, talking soldiers to him won't be my first priority.'

'I understand. He must have survived that shackling. I wonder what happened to his brother?'

That was one of the questions in my mind, though not the most important. I'd come to trust Sheila and had resolved the concern about Szabo. I was off the hook on the steroids charge and should have been able to concentrate on Cassidy/Cummings and his links with Patrick. But now I had a question about Casey. He seemed to have everything he needed, so why the naked ambition? Wasn't professor as high as you could go before becoming a bean-counting bureaucrat?

23

I replied to Angela Warburton, saying that I'd be glad to see
her when she came to Sydney. I said I hadn't been in the surf
for fifteen years but was prepared to give it a go if I could find
a board long enough. What I didn't say was that I'd have to
get in some practice first.

Sheila got back from Melbourne excited by what she'd
picked up about criminal matriarchs. We celebrated her return
in the usual ways. She gave me an impromptu performance
of one of the scenes in the script and was very good. Chilling.
She asked me what I'd been doing and I told her just about
everything. We were in bed on a cold morning, reluctant to
get up for the run to the bathroom.

She drew closer. 'Jesus, Seamus a mercenary and an
assassin. It's hard to believe.'

'It's not proven yet.'

'It sounds like something out of Frederick Forsyth.

What're you going to do?'

'I'm going down to Kangaroo Valley with this Jack Casey to hunt him out.'

'Shouldn't you go to the police?'

I hadn't said anything about the security services angle. Now I did.

'It sounds like something out of le Carré.'

'It won't be. If he killed Patrick it'll be for some mundane reason, probably money. No glamour, no ideology.'

'Now it sounds dangerous.'

'Casey's ex-SAS. We'll be all right.'

We got up and had breakfast; at least I did. Sheila, noticeably thinner, was still watching the carbs and had black coffee.

'Be careful your kidneys don't shut down,' I said.

'Always with the jokes. Can we be serious for a minute?'

I thought I knew what was coming and I realised that I hadn't thought enough about it. A mistake I'd made too many times before. Good times, good sex, what next? But I was wrong.

Sheila finished her coffee and dabbed at her mouth, careful not to smudge the faint lip-gloss. She'd bought clothes in Melbourne and was looking terrific in a red cashmere sweater, black trousers and medium-heel boots. She was less heavily made-up than before with more lines showing. She looked mature, experienced and all the more sexy for it.

'I want to come with you,' she said.

'I don't think so.'

'He'd talk to me. I'm sure he would. He might not talk to you. From what you say he just might shoot you.'

'We'll make sure that doesn't happen.'

'So you'll make it safe. What's the objection then? You tracked him under the name of Cummings, right?'

'It helped.'

'I put you on to that, Cliff. You owe me.'

'It's not a movie.'

'Don't insult me. I know it's not a movie, but it's about my ex-lover perhaps being the murderer of my husband. I've got a stake in this. You say you want to know why. I bloody well want to know, too.'

I thought back to when I suspected she could have been in it for the money and could have been lying about still being married to Patrick. I'd come full circle on those points. She'd barely mentioned Patrick's estate since that first encounter, and she had been helpful. It went against every instinct to take her, but my instincts have been wrong before. Perhaps she could help on the spot.

'You're wavering.'

'What if I say no?'

'I'll be pissed off, and I'll think you're lacking in . . .'

'What?'

She shrugged. 'I don't know. Something.'

She didn't know it, but she had me cold. I wanted her with me; it was as simple as that. Or almost. What I'd said before about exorcising Patrick held true even more now. I didn't know what Casey would think of it, but I was running things, wasn't I?

'Okay,' I said.

'Thank you.'

'You're crazy,' Jack Casey said when we met again in the Balmain pub.

I'd thought my excuse out beforehand. 'She had me over a barrel,' I said, giving him the whiskey. 'If I hadn't agreed she said she'd go to the police and tell them everything we knew.'

'That'd stuff it for sure. Why'd you tell her in the first place? Sorry, shouldn't have said that. Not my business.'

'That's all right. She matters to me and she's part of it.'

He nodded and we went on to the details of our expedition. I'd emailed the Aussie Irish Travellers' website with details of my Malloy grandmother and my interest in attending the gathering in the company of Sheila Malloy and John Casey. There was a two hundred dollar a head registration fee to cover administrative expenses and a dinner: I paid by credit card. Attendees who wished could camp at the farm. There were also a limited number of powered sites available on a first-come-first-served basis. A block booking at the Valley Caravan and Cabin Park had ensured cut-rate accommodation for others.

'Cold down there this time of year,' Casey said.

'Take a sleeping bag. You can sleep in that bloody huge SUV you drove up in. Sheila and me'll get a cabin. We can make you coffee and a hot water bottle—two hot water bottles.'

Casey smiled. 'Fuck you,' he said.

A good start.

'What d'you think of him?' I asked Sheila following a brief meeting with Casey before we left for Kangaroo Valley. He was still waiting for a message from his informant about the photo of the mercenaries. I had a niggling worry that if Casey and Sheila got to talking he'd find out that I'd lied to him about her threatening to tell all to the cops.

'Too soon to tell.'

It was a two-hour drive. Casey drove his SUV and Sheila and I followed in the Falcon. We skirted the 'Gong, went west at Nowra, and began the climb before dropping down into the valley.

'I came here once years ago,' Sheila said. 'Bloke I was with had an old rust-bucket Holden with a dodgy clutch. He had to go up one of these steep hills in reverse.'

'Yeah? I remember that sort of thing—old bombs with no starter motor so you had to park on a slope; broken wind-screen wipers you had to work with a couple of bits of string. All gone now.'

'And good riddance.'

'I suppose so.'

'Come on, they were death traps, those cars.'

An Alfa Romeo passed us at speed on the steep road, rounding a blind bend. 'Those aren't?'

'Seatbelts, child restraints, breathalysers—it's all better.'

'You're right. I drove lots of times right across Sydney half pissed when I was young.'

'Only half?'

'Okay, two-thirds. Jack's going to get there well ahead of us. Let's stop for the view.'

We detoured to the lookout on Cambewarra Mountain. There was a view east across Nowra to the ocean and west across the valley. We stood at the rail, wrapped in our coats and with our arms around each other.

'Nice,' Sheila said. 'You ever fancy a sea change, Cliff?'

'Yeah, sure—Bondi, Coogee, even Watsons Bay.'

She laughed. 'That'd be right.'

By arrangement, we met Casey outside the Visitors Centre in the township where he was studying a brochure and a map and puffing on a cigar. Sheila sniffed the aroma and a look of longing crossed her face.

'The farm's about eight k's out of town on Bendeela Road,' he said, 'and the caravan park's on the same road a bit closer. Of course we've got the option of staying somewhere more flash. What d'you reckon?'

Sheila said, 'Seamus is a campin', huntin', shootin' and fishin' type, or was. I think he'd be in a tent.'

'Doesn't sound like your type, Sheila,' Casey said.

I could see his point. Sheila wore a suede three-quarter length coat over her red sweater, a stylish scarf, designer cords and boots.

'I was younger and I could fuck in a sleeping bag with the best of them, Jack. Blow that smoke away, would you please? I quit recently.'

'We'll go to the farm and register,' I said. 'Maybe we can find out where Cummings is staying. He might have changed his habits. With luck it could be one of these resort joints. I'm not anxious to rough it. Weather looks iffy.'

The clear morning light was dimming with dark clouds gathering to the east.

'Maybe we should have hired a couple of caravans or mobile homes and stayed at the farm,' Casey said.

I shook my head. 'I doubt we could pass as the real thing. I saw these Travellers in Ireland—they've got a particular style. Not gypsy exactly, but not grey nomad either. That's what you and I'd look like, Jack.'

'And me,' Sheila said, 'but for superb hair product.'

Casey, who'd been carefully blowing his smoke away from her, gave Sheila an approving nod. 'You tell it how it is, don't you?'

'Always,' Sheila said. 'And what exactly are you planning to do?'

'We'll decide that when we find him,' I said. 'We've got no proof he's our man. We'll have to see what he does and hear what he says.'

'Circumstantial proof,' Casey said. 'Anyway, my intentions and Cliff's aren't the same. I want to know if he was a member of the Olympic Corps.'

I don't know why, but for some reason when I'd told Sheila about our investigation and assumptions, I hadn't mentioned the name of the mercenary unit.

She snapped her fingers. 'That's it. That's what he called it. I'm quite sure. I can smell . . .'

'Smell what?' I said.

'Jesus, that triggered it. He said he'd just come back from New Caledonia. In the Pacific. He was smoking Gitanes. I had one.'

Smell sets off memory, usually painful in my experience, better than almost anything else. And memory sets off emotion. Sheila leaned against me.

'I'm not so sure now that I want to do this,' she said.

Casey dropped his cigar on the ground and put his foot on it. 'This is amazing,' he said. 'There was a big blow-up in New Caledonia twenty years ago and talk of mercenaries being recruited. Didn't come to anything much. I have to talk to this guy.'

Sheila had lost colour and was staring up the road, not seeing anything, looking as if she wanted to be almost anywhere else.

'It's all right, love,' I said. 'I'll find us somewhere you can have a rest. Jack, I . . .'

I turned around. The cigar butt was still smoking but Casey had gone.

24

I booked Sheila into one of the township's motels.

'Sorry to wimp out on you,' she said.

'It's all right. No one likes to relive the bad times.'

'They *were* bad times. I was a mess back then, booze and drugs and blokes, and remembering that name just sort of brought it all back. Why did Jack take off like that?'

'I don't know, but I have to find out.'

'Sure you do. Just be careful. I'll hunker down here for a while. Maybe get some DVDs and keep doing my crunches. Call me if I can help. Promise?'

I drove straight to the farm, passing the caravan park on the way. The drought of the past few years seemed not to have affected the valley; the rolling landscape was a patchwork of lush paddocks with dairy cattle grazing. Under other circumstances the expedition would have been an interesting experience. Caravans and mobile homes and campervans were clustered around a magnificent old sandstone farmhouse. An area was set aside for tents and heavy-duty cables snaked across the ground, providing power. I could hear the thrum of a couple of generators as I got out of the car and approached the house. No sign of Casey's vehicle.

A reception area was set up on the wide front verandah with a brazier burning nearby. Early afternoon, but it was cold already with a cloudy sky and a stiff wind. A woman sat on a bench behind a table with a list in front of her and a stack of brightly coloured plastic folders and name tags on strings. People sat on chairs on the verandah or leaned against the rail, smoking and yarning. In a way they resembled the sorts of people you'd expect to find at Tamworth for the country music festival—jeans, hats, boots. But the women tended to wear more beads and bangles, like the hippies of old, and a lot of the men were fleshy, not going for the lean cowboy look.

I presented my driver's licence to the woman at the table.

She ran her heavily ringed finger down her list. 'Welcome, Mr Hardy. You're a Malloy, I see.'

'That's right.'

'I'm Molly Maguire and here's your kit and name tag. Inside you'll find the events planned and a ticket to the dinner. I see you booked for two other people.'

'Yes. My partner Sheila's not well. She's staying in town

for now but I'll take her kit. She'll be up and about soon. Has Jack Casey checked in?'

'Sorry to hear that about your lady friend.' She studied her list. 'No, not yet.'

'How about Seamus Cummings? Old mate of mine. I'm anxious to catch up with him.'

'Hmm, yes, he registered earlier today.'

'Did he say where he was staying?'

'Oh, I remember him now. He didn't look well. He said he'd be getting a cabin at the caravan park. They're quite comfortable, I believe.'

'D'you know what he was driving?'

One question too many. She looked suspicious and automatically glanced across to where I'd parked my car. 'And where are you staying?'

I gave her one of my smiles. 'Sorry to be so nosy. Doesn't matter. I'm at the caravan park.'

The smile and the apology brought her round. 'It's just that you sounded a bit official. Not too keen on officials, us Travellers.'

'Right. They told me in Ireland officials put bars up at a certain height on the car parks to prevent the Travellers bringing in their vans and trailers.'

'Oh, have you been there?'

'Very recently. I met up with quite a few Malloys.'

That won her over. 'Perhaps you might give us a little talk about your trip.'

Not likely, I thought, but I smiled again and nodded as I picked up my kit and Sheila's and moved away.

'Mr Malloy . . .'

I turned back. 'Hardy.'

'I'm sorry. Your friend Mr Cummings should be at the caravan park by now. I'm sure you'll be able to find him.'

And so can Jack Casey, I thought. The idea of Casey operating on his own worried me. We had different priorities, as he'd said. In a way he was as obsessed by mercenaries as Patrick had been by the Travellers. To get the inside track on the Olympic Corps could do him an enormous amount of good professionally. Mercenaries being killers by definition, Casey had had dealings with men with blood on their hands in his research. In fact it might've been part of the attraction. The fact that Cummings was probably a murderer as a civilian was something Casey should be able to take in his stride.

I drove to the caravan park and asked if Cummings and Casey had checked in. They had, both taking cabins.

'Will you be staying, sir?' the manager, a beefy, hearty type in a flannie and beanie asked.

'Not sure. I'd like a word with them first. Can you give me the numbers of their cabins?'

'Thirty-one for the 4WD and thirty-three for the ute, in the third row. Better make up your mind. Them gypsies is coming in fast.'

Patrick, who would have loved the idea of the gathering,

wouldn't have liked to hear that. I left my car outside the park and walked in along the gravel road. It was an orderly and well-maintained establishment. The cabins were laid out in rows, about ten in each, probably sixty plus all up. An adjacent area was set aside for powered sites to be used by cars or vans and there were a few tents over in a corner close to what looked like a shower and laundry block.

Some of the cabins had occupants, most didn't, but there were signs that they were taken—boxes, boots and sneakers on the porches, clothes on the retractable lines. I did a careful reconnoitre: cabin 33, Cummings's, was the third last in the row; Casey's was the last. I had my hands in my pockets, just strolling around, but I had a feeling of being vulnerable and an unusual sensation of wishing I was armed.

A Holden ute was parked near Cummings's cabin, 33, but there was no sign of Casey's SUV. I walked away thinking that this was all wrong. To the extent that we'd had a plan, our idea was to locate Cummings, watch him and decide what to do when we'd sussed him out. Casey's jumping the gun had blown that out of the water.

A golf cart came trundling down the road, driven by the manager. He pulled up beside me.

'Thought I should tell you, mate, that there's only two spots left. And I just remembered that I saw the two blokes you was asking about driving off in the big 4WD a bit before you showed up. Slipped my mind, being so busy, like.'

It sometimes happens. I had absolutely no idea what to do next. Had Casey gone willingly? For that matter, had Cummings gone willingly? In either case, where? And why? With a vehicle like that, there were very few places in the whole bloody country they couldn't go. I rang Casey's mobile and was told that the phone had either been switched off or was not contactable.

I left a message: *Jack, Cliff. Where are you and what're you doing? Call me.*

Couldn't put it any plainer than that.

I drove back to the township and the motel. I knocked, said her name, and Sheila let me in. The room was warm and she'd stripped down to a spencer and her trousers. She grabbed me, pulled me inside, and we kissed. She had a classical music concert playing at low volume on the TV, a bottle of white wine open and a newspaper folded to show the cryptic crossword. She broke away, went to the mini-bar for a glass and waved at the bottle. I nodded and she poured.

'How're you feeling?' I said.

'I'm fine. It was just an emotional glitch. I go up and down a bit as you've probably noticed. I wasn't expecting you back so soon but I'm glad. Is there anything lonelier than a motel room on your own?'

'No. Absolutely not.'

She picked up her glass. 'So, what's happening? What're you doing?'

I told her in detail, partly to straighten things out in my

own mind. When I finished I said, 'In answer to your second question, I haven't the faintest bloody idea.'

'Maybe something'll come to you. Meanwhile, let's not waste this nice warm room and comfy bed.'

We made love. She dozed while I stared at the ceiling trying to work out what might have happened. As Sheila had said, Cummings looked unnaturally thin in the Irish photograph and the woman at the farm said he looked ill. Casey was solid and strong. I'd back him in a physical contest against a man who appeared to be in poor heath. But there was the matter of a shotgun and experience. You'd have to back a veteran of the Irish troubles and the Angolan civil war over a cotton-wooled Gulf War I participant.

Sheila stirred and came awake. She saw me staring into space and elbowed me lightly in the ribs. 'I've remembered something.'

'Mmm?'

'I don't think Paddy ever mentioned anything about this Irish Traveller stuff . . .'

'I think he only found out about it after you split.'

'. . . but Seamus did. He knew about it. He told me about moving around in Ireland from one place to another. Something about dogs and horses. He said he missed it. I think I made fun of it, said something about gypsies, and he got angry. He did that a lot—got angry. I gave him reason, but he was angry by nature. Which made him exciting, back then, as screwed up as I was.'

'Well, I gather they had a hard time, the Travellers, until fairly recently. A sort of minority. The kids' education would've been buggered up, and Ireland was in a mess until the IT and the tax people got together.'

'Yes, but the point is, he's come here for this gathering and paid good money for it. And you say he looks unwell but he came anyway. If he's got any say in it, I reckon he'd be at this dinner. Don't you?'

25

It seemed a reasonable assumption, and it was the only one we had to work with. We had our tickets to the dinner and surely there was safety in numbers. If Cummings showed up at the dinner he was hardly likely to cause trouble with so many people around. Also, to judge by the men I'd seen out at the farm and the few arriving at the caravan park as I left, there were some pretty formidable faces and bodies among them.

I moved into Sheila's room with my baggage and we set about making ourselves presentable for the evening. We showered; Sheila dealt with her hair and face while I shaved. The event was bound to be far from formal, but Molly Maguire had been pretty dolled up with rings and with little mirrors on her skirt and her velvet jacket, so I guessed people would go in a certain amount of style. Best I could do was a clean white linen shirt, black

PETER CORRIS

slacks and shoes and a newish olive jacket. Sheila teamed
her boots with black velvet pants, her red sweater and
a jacket with silver threads running through it. She wrapped
her scarf round her neck and paraded for me.

'What d'you reckon?'

'Can you flamenco?'

'If I have to. How about you?'

'Love, I can barely waltz. Jive a bit if I'm pissed enough.
Come to think of it, I know your married and stage names but
not your maiden name. Don't tell me it's Kelly or Higgins.'

'Fitzsimmons; Cornish. My great-great-something grandfather was transported for smuggling.'

'Good for him,' I said.

'Jesus, it's like night football,' Sheila said.

The lights were visible from a kilometre away. The road
to the gate and the area around the farmhouse were lit up
and the building itself glowed like a beacon. An attendant
directed the car to a parking area and we joined a troop of
people heading for the house. The women, of all shapes and
sizes, wore colourful dresses, skirts and blouses, nothing
drab. I was more or less in tune sartorially with the older men
except for one thing—no hat. Hats and caps were in—green,
white, black, red—and feathers were popular as well.

We presented our tickets at the door and were ushered
by a young woman, in a floor-length dress and jangling

212

bangles, around the verandah to the back of the house. The wide verandah had been built in to form a long room with trestle tables and chairs down the centre. There looked to be seating for a couple of hundred, with place cards propped up beside the cutlery and a very encouraging array of bottles. About half the places were already occupied with more people flooding in, and the noise level was going up. The background music, fiddles and pipes and drums, was battling against the chatter and the clink of glasses and bottles. The air was smoky. Potbelly stoves at either end of the room were dealing with the chill.

'Like the old days,' Sheila said, 'when you could have a smoke with your tucker.'

'Problem for you?'

'We'll see. Anyway, this could be fun.'

The band was grouped at the end of the room on a raised platform. Three men and two women with a variety of instruments in use and others propped up waiting to be played. The girl who'd brought us in had a list and she directed us to seats near the middle of the room. We sat down with a pair of Hennessys next to me and an ancient Clancy next to Sheila. The protocol was printed on the place card: *Say 'Buri talosk' to your neighbour, shake hands or kiss, fill your glass and toast each other*. We did, me with Guinness, Sheila with red wine. I squinted through the haze. If it got much worse, I'd have trouble seeing people at either end of the table, but, so far, there was no sign of Seamus Cummings.

We went through the ritual, chatted to each other, the people on either side, and the ones opposite. The menu featured leek and potato soup, casseroled rabbit and apple pie. The wines were all cleanskins from the Hunter Valley. The Guinness ran out quickly before the soup arrived. I tried not to be looking too obviously as the places filled up. There were bound to be no-shows for one reason or another, but there were only about five or six chairs unoccupied when the music stopped and a man identified by the old fellow next to me as Corey O'Loughlin, our host, got up and announced the order of business. There was to be a welcoming address at the end of the first course by himself and a short speech about the history of the Irish Travellers in Australia by Dr Brian O'Keefe . . .

'And then youse can dig into the apple pie and the sweet wine and dance the calories off as we clear the room.'

There were cheers, hoots and hollers as the band struck up again. O'Loughlin was a two-metre giant, built in proportion. I couldn't help watching him as he drained a glass, took up a fiddle and joined the band. When I looked back at the table I saw Seamus Cummings, deeply tanned, skeletally thin, sitting on the opposite side a few seats away, staring at Sheila, who was deep in conversation with the woman next to her. When she stopped to take a drink she saw Cummings. She could hardly miss him, his gaze seemed to send out a beam of hot light.

Sheila turned to me. 'He looks like death.'

She didn't mean deadly. Cummings was much thinner than when I'd seen him in Ireland. His shirt and jacket hung loosely on his bony torso and his hands around a glass of wine were like thin, brown, articulated sticks. He nodded at Sheila who nodded back. He shot me a look that was hard to interpret—indifference, or contempt—and turned his attention to his food.

Sheila had finished her soup and just pushed the rabbit around on the plate. I'd eaten half of mine but now I lost all appetite.

'What do we do?' Sheila whispered.

'We wait.'

It was difficult not to stare at Cummings, who seemed to have abandoned interest in us and was listening to what his neighbour was saying while alternating bites of his food with sips of his wine. He nodded and smiled and the smile was ghastly in that fleshless face.

The music stopped and the gigantic O'Loughlin called for quiet in a roaring voice none would disobey. He introduced the small, dapper man at the top table as Brian O'Keefe and yielded the floor to him.

I can't say that I took in a word of what O'Keefe said. I was aware of laughter and people nodding in agreement and an occasional clap, but my mind was fully occupied with two questions: *Where was Jack Casey and what was Cummings likely to do?*

O'Keefe finished and sat down. The apple pie and cream

arrived and the talk started up, louder as some of the diners got oiled and competed with the music. Plates cleaned, mouths wiped, people began to get up from the table and drift away to form groups. The music picked up pace and started to sound like the introduction to a jig. Cummings levered himself up slowly and walked to the end of the table. I stood but he gestured for me to stay where I was as he approached, bracing himself now and then on the backs of chairs. He reached us and stood, wheezing and sucking in the smoky air.

'Hello, Sheila, old darlin'. You're looking well.'

Sheila had stayed sitting. 'Hello, Seamus.'

He smiled. 'You don't think I'm looking well?'

Sheila said nothing. Cummings was as tall as me and he looked me straight in the eye.

'Cliff Hardy,' he said. 'You have the misfortune to closely resemble a piece of shite named Paddy Malloy.'

'I resent that,' I said. 'He was my cousin and yes, I did look like him.'

'That's right, you did. Cousin, is it? If I was to tell you about the cousins I've lost . . . Now I suggest you two have a little dance. I'd ask you, Sheila, but I'm a bit past the dancin' myself. I'll just watch, and if I see you leaving or making telephone calls, you'll not see your bearded professor friend ever again.'

'Where is he, Cummings?'

Cummings smiled and did a little, jerky jig, as if warming

up for a dance he'd never complete. 'Now, now, have a little patience. You've taken a lot of trouble and some time to reach this point, Hardy. Just be patient a while and you'll learn all you want to know.'

26

It's an old trick—you get the people you're trying to control to do something they don't want to do, just for starters. I stood my ground with my hand on Sheila's shoulder.

'Fuck you,' I said. 'Get on with whatever you've got in your sick mind.'

That death's-head smile again. 'I'm sick all right, but my mind's as clear as a Galway stream. Just stay with me—the threat remains the same.'

The organisers were clearing away the trestles and chairs and the remainder of the food and drink, and the musicians were refreshing themselves before their next onslaught. People were gathering in groups ready to dance. Cummings backed away carefully, taking small steps. The healthy tan was deceptive; his sunken eyes were pools of pain as he moved and his hands shook as he took a mobile phone from his pocket. He reached the wall and steadied himself, fighting for breath. Sheila and I moved with him, keeping a couple of metres away as he sent a text message.

'You're very sick, Seamus,' Sheila said. 'You need help.'

He put the phone away. 'I'm beyond help, darlin', but I've done the two things I needed to do so it doesn't matter a tinker's curse.'

A paroxysm of coughing shook him; his knees sagged but he fought to keep himself upright. This was a very determined man.

'Let's go,' he said when he'd recovered. 'I just have to say goodbye to Mr O'Loughlin, fine man that he is.'

Painfully slowly, Cummings approached O'Loughlin, who was loading wood into the potbelly stove near the band. O'Loughlin saw him and straightened up.

'Long live the Travellers of whom I'm a proud member. Sorry I can't stay longer, but I'm broken down in body as you see, but not in spirit.'

O'Loughlin took Cummings's outstretched hand in the gentlest of holds and put his other hand lightly on his shoulder. The contrast between the two men could not have been greater—O'Loughlin must have weighed 120 kilos and Cummings looked to have wasted away to about half that and, although Cummings was tall, O'Loughlin topped him by a head. Sheila and I hung back.

'My name is Seamus Cummings of County Galway. I want to thank you, Mr O'Loughlin, for a fine evening and to say *slán*.'

'*Slán* to you, Seamus, and may God bless you.'

'I doubt that, but thank you.'

Cummings turned towards us as O'Loughlin gave us a salute—the gallant support staff. Cummings looked about to fall and I couldn't do anything but step forward and take his arm. We left the room as the band struck up and the so-inclined Travellers swung into their dance. We reached the door and Cummings, feather light, turned to take a last look. I heard a sniff from Sheila and when I looked I saw her dabbing at a tear with the sleeve of her jacket.

Jesus, I thought, *this man murdered her husband and my friend. What the hell is going on here?*

We shuffled along and I couldn't tell whether Cummings was as decrepit as he seemed. He'd appeared to be all right when he took his seat and while he was eating and drinking. I strongly suspected that, weak though he undoubtedly was, he'd play on his appearance for any advantage he could get.

Bottles empty and not empty had been stacked on a sideboard in the hallway and Cummings suddenly pulled free of me.

'Better pick up a few,' he said. 'We've paid for it after all, and we've got a long night and a lot of talking ahead of us.'

I picked up three bottles. Sheila seemed to be moving in a trance-like state. Cummings noticed.

'For Christ's sake, Sheila,' he rasped. 'Grab a bottle or two. What's wrong with you?'

Sheila's head came up and she moved quickly to block his

path. 'Grab them yourself, Seamus. It's a long time since I did what you told me.'

'Did at one time though, didn't you, darlin'? And loved it.'

'Knock it off,' I said. 'We're not going one step further until you tell us what's going on.'

'How about your friend?'

'He's not a friend. He's someone I used to help track you down.'

'Is that a fact? He'll be disappointed to hear it. We drove about a bit and got on famously. I told him some things he didn't know and helped him sort out the dirty lies from the dirty truths.'

'The blarney is giving me the shits. Who did you send the text to?'

'Ah, good question. Just the right question. I can see that you have a brain in your head. Well, I might say the same as you. He's no friend of mine but someone I've found useful. I think we may have more in common than it looks, Hardy.'

'If it's the right question, what's the answer?'

Cummings laughed and the movement brought on another spell of coughing and forced him to lean against a wall again. 'He . . . he's by way of being a member of the Australian intelligence service, oxymoron though that is, and he's known about me and Patrick Malloy and you and your friend Casey for days and days and days. And I know about him, so I thought to invite him along to a little meeting.

Not a *céilidh*, mind, Hardy, but you'll want to be there for certain.'

We followed Cummings in his black ute away from the farm.

'I hope you've got that gun with you,' Sheila said.

'I haven't, it was a temporary measure.'

As I expected, Cummings turned in at the caravan park. I drove past.

'What're you doing?'

'Taking you back to the motel.'

'You do and I'll never fucking speak to you again.'

'Sheila, he's a killer.'

'Maybe he was, but not now. You saw and heard him. The man's on his last legs. He wants to talk. I'm involved in this, Cliff. I want to see it through.'

She had a point. I slowed down. 'I don't like the sound of the intelligence people being involved. A minute ago you were wishing I had a gun.'

'I was dramatising. It's one of my faults. How can it hurt to have a security guy there? Look, I meant what I said, Cliff. I like you a lot. I think we could be good together, but I'm buggered if I'll be sidelined. Turn around . . . please.'

I did. It wasn't late and the boom gate hadn't come down. The place was fairly well lit and I remembered the layout well enough to navigate back to cabins 31 and 33. The black ute was there, parked next to 33 with Casey's SUV by 31. The porch light was on at 33 and Cummings stood at the door wrapped in a blanket. His breath steamed in the cold air. We drew up behind the SUV and got out, Sheila carrying one bottle and me two.

'We were waiting for the grog. Lose your way, did you?'

His grin showed that he knew exactly what had happened. I didn't give him the satisfaction of a reply. 'Jack?' I called.

'Careful, you'll wake the neighbours,' Cummings said.

Casey appeared behind Cummings. He looked strained and white as he puffed nervously on a cigar. A movement behind him suggested there was someone else inside.

'Better get in here, Cliff. Tell Sheila to wait in the car.'

'Dunno about that, Jack. She'd be likely to ram your vehicle and then have a go at the cabin. That'd wake the neighbours.'

'That's right,' Sheila said. 'Fuck you, Jack.'

'All in together then,' Cummings said. 'It'll be a little cramped, but who looks for a lot of room at a good party, eh?'

Cummings and Casey eased back inside and Sheila and I went up two steps to the porch and through the door. The cabin was bigger inside than it looked from outside. There was a kitchenette and doors to what I assumed to be a bathroom and sleeping area. A table stood in the middle of the room, and there was space for four chairs around it and two armchairs in the corners. An oil heater was keeping the place warm.

Jack Casey sat at the table. Cummings eased himself into one of the armchairs. The other was occupied by a pale man with thinning ginger hair. He wore a suit and tie and stood as we entered to offer the chair to Sheila, smoothing down his tie as he did so. Sheila shook her head. We deposited the bottles on the table where they joined a half-full bottle of Johnny Walker red. Casey had an empty glass in front of him and the other man had a glass at his feet.

'This is Martin Milton-Smith,' Cummings said. 'He's by way of being with ASIS, isn't that right, Martin?'

Milton-Smith subsided back into his chair and reached for his glass. 'Something like that.'

'Something like that,' Cummings repeated.

'We've met,' I said. 'You visited Pat in hospital.'

'That's right.'

'I didn't like the look of you then anymore than I do now. I should've asked Pat who you were, but that was back when I thought I knew who *he* was.'

Cummings moved the scotch bottle an inch. 'I don't like to mix my drinks and I fancy a drop of that good wine we had tonight. Would you care to fetch a couple of glasses, Hardy?'

He was at it again, running the show. I pulled out a chair for Sheila and then opened both the other doors, switched on the lights and looked inside. Both empty.

I sat and said, 'I think Jack could get the glasses. Probably knows where they are, same layout as his cabin.'

'Good point,' Cummings said.

Still without speaking, Casey got up and brought three tumblers from the kitchenette.

'I'm for the red,' Cummings said. 'Sheila? Hardy?'

I poured him a glass of red and one for myself. Sheila waved a refusal.

'Okay, Seamus,' I said. 'You've had your fun. Now let's hear what this is all about.'

'I think I should step in here,' Milton-Smith said, 'just to bring you up to date as it were. We've had a watching brief on Professor Casey for some time, ever since his research started to touch on matters of national security. He has been very careful but apparently he was carried away by information brought to him by you, Mr Hardy. We've been able to monitor his emails and telephone calls.'

'I hope you're proud of yourselves,' I said.

'It's not a matter for pride, simply of doing what has to be done. Anyway, we tracked you and Professor Casey here which led us to Mr Cummings, in whom we have a special interest.'

'And that's a black lie,' Cummings said. 'I've been doing more tracking than being tracked. I invited you here, remember.'

'I think we know why,' Milton-Smith murmured.

'I don't. What's all this "we" business?' I said. 'You make it sound as if you've got spooks hiding behind every rubbish bin.'

'Not quite, but certain assets are in place.'

'That sort of language makes you a laughing-stock,' Sheila said.

'I don't think you'll be laughing by the time we finish here, Ms Fitzsimmons. Mr Cummings . . .?'

Cummings took a big swallow of the red, cleared his throat and drew in a deep breath. 'Most people don't know what a shite hole Angola was all through the seventies and eighties. They'd no sooner got their independence from Portugal when they started fighting each other under different names— MPLA, FLNA, UNITA—it was like something out of *The Life of Brian*, except that it wasn't funny. They reckon forty thousand people were killed and about a million were made homeless in the first couple of weeks.

'Then the Soviets and the Cubans hopped in with tanks and planes and the slaughter went on and on. Those bloody Africans hate each other worse than they hate us, and they hate us like poison. The different sides started to enlist mercenaries—a few of them got themselves topped in '76, but they were just the ones the media picked up. Hostages were being taken every other day and murdered and mercenaries, a lot of them undocumented in the sort of language Martin likes, just fuckin' disappeared. This went on well into the eighties when the world's attention had switched elsewhere. Some of those militia leaders who felt they'd missed out on the goodies or had axes to grind were getting dollops of money from here and there and still recruiting.'

'Ratbag people like the Olympic Corps,' I said.

Cummings showed more emotion than he had so far. 'I know where you got that, from Paddy Malloy. All fuckin' wrong. It was an elite group. The best.'

Couldn't buck that sincerity. 'Okay,' I said.

'You can't imagine what it was like fighting in that country. Just existing's hard enough. The border with the Congo was like a sieve, anyone could get across and the Congo River, in case you don't know, has these heavily wooded islands in it you can hide in, retreat to, attack river traffic from. Angola's all fuckin' mountains when it isn't swamp and jungle. Insects to eat you alive, elephant grass to slice you to bits. Malaria . . . anyway, we were fighting for this splinter group from the MPLA faction that pretty well had everyone else against it. Did well, too, scored some heavy hits.'

The energy seemed to drain out of him. He drank some wine, took a pill bottle from his pocket, shook some pills into his palm and took them with another gulp of wine. There was no blarney now, no performance. He was living the experience.

'We were betrayed and ambushed. We lost two good men and twelve of us were taken. There were four Australians in the team including Malloy, but he was a plant, working for UNITA.'

'And for his country,' Milton-Smith said.

'Oh, that's right. Your government was very opposed to any of its citizens being mercenaries. Happy for them to fight for the fuckin' Brits and Americans anywhere in the world, but not for themselves. Not for filthy lucre.'

'Not for communists,' Milton-Smith said.

Cummings ignored him. 'He betrayed us. We were hauled off to a bush jail and I'm telling you Guantanamo Bay and Abu Ghraib're picnic spots compared to that. We were beaten and starved and raped. My brother, a year younger than me, was beaten to death, slowly, right in front of me.'

'What happened to you, Seamus?' Sheila said.

'Oh, I was beaten, too, and shot and buried, but I survived, after a fashion. I spent some time with decomposing corpses. It hurts your mind as well as your body and it's something people like you wouldn't know anything about. I got back on my feet for a while, as you know, Sheila, but it all caught up with me in the end. This fuckin' cancer came as no surprise. I lived just to come face to face with Paddy Malloy and I came to Australia time and time again to look for him, but I never found him.'

'That's why you freaked out when you saw my picture of him,' Sheila said.

'Right, darlin'. I missed my chance then. I got drunk and went to jail and when I got out you'd gone and he'd gone and I was back where I started.'

'How did you know Paddy betrayed you?' Sheila said.

'I can answer that,' Milton-Smith said. 'He tortured a man to death to get the information about Malloy. Very nasty.'

'And then you saw him at the Ballintrath *céilidh*,' I said.

'I did and it was a sweet moment. He didn't see me. He was too busy dancing and he was too pissed. I made myself scarce, but I knew him at once. I've kept tabs on you and him ever since. Missed you here and there but I picked you up again. I've had some help.'

I shook my head and he laughed.

'Don't get upset, Hardy. I had professional help. Better than you or maybe just younger. Fuck it. Paddy Malloy killed my comrades and my brother and left me a wreck and that's why I did for him in a way he'd understand. I'd do it again. I wish to Christ I *could* do it again.'

27

Cummings's head was bowed and he was crying quietly.

'I told Paddy about the Travellers, him being a Malloy and all, when we . . . when I thought we were comrades,' he said through his tears. 'He didn't know much about it and he was interested. It was like a double betrayal, d'you see?'

Sheila shuffled her chair along and put her hand on Cummings's shoulder. 'Why didn't you leave the country after you'd killed Paddy? It was so risky to stay.'

Cummings sniffed and blinked away the tears. 'Nothing's risky for a man in my condition, darlin'. I had some old friends to see and I really wanted to go to this gathering. Just to be there, to see the faces and hear the music.'

'Touching,' Milton-Smith said, 'but the fact remains that you murdered an Australian intelligence agent.'

'So arrest me,' Cummings said. 'The fuck do I care? I'm a dead man walking.' He smiled and lifted his tear-stained face to look at Sheila. 'Sitting, that is.'

Milton-Smith stood and poured himself a small measure of scotch. 'True, it was all a good time back, but we can't have it getting out that an Australian intelligence agency conspired to have some of our citizens . . . eliminated. However delinquent they may have been. There were a couple of Australians in that merry band, recruited by the Cummings brothers. The good professor didn't pick them up in his research.'

I was getting tired of Milton-Smith and I was angry with Casey, whose carelessness had let the spooks into the picture. 'I hope you're getting all this down on your cleverly concealed tape recorder, Jack,' I said.

Casey stirred for the first time since our arrival. Fumbling, he relit his cigar that had gone out and puffed smoke at Milton-Smith. 'I'm sorry, Cliff. I've screwed everything up badly. This bastard has me by the balls.'

'In a manner of speaking,' Milton-Smith said. 'Professor Casey has been indiscreet, we find, with one or two of his students. His career is in my hands, rather than his balls.'

I'd been in a similar situation once before, when the spooks had stepped into an investigation and tied it all up in a way that suited them and left me, and others, no room for manoeuvre.

'So tell us about the cover-up,' I said, 'and why we all have to go along with it.'

'I wouldn't put it quite that way,' Milton-Smith said.

'I'd rather say that, in the interest of national security and the reputation of some of our valued institutions, certain arrangements have to be made.'

Sheila laughed. 'Meaning you're going to cover up a murder.'

'They've already started to do that,' I said. 'They closed down the police investigation. Isn't that right, Martin?'

Milton-Smith took a sip of his scotch, enjoying himself. 'An example of what I said, arrangements being made.'

Sheila said, 'I can see why Jack's going to keep quiet about it, but . . .'

Milton-Smith began to tick points off—right index finger against left thumb. 'Let me make it clear, then. One, I doubt that Mr Cummings wants to spend his few remaining weeks in a prison hospital. In fact I happen to know he has excellent palliative care all lined up. Very sensible. Two, the film you're hoping to work on, Ms Fitzsimmons, dealing as it does with actual events and characters, doesn't quite have all its financing in place. Close, but not quite. It can also be subject to legal injunctions that would delay or frustrate it altogether. Do you follow?'

'You bastard,' Sheila said. 'What about Cliff? He's got media contacts. He could blow the story wide open.'

'Ah, yes, Mr Hardy, defrocked private enquiry agent who's already served time in prison for serious offences and who allegedly imported dangerous substances into this country. If convicted, he'd be looking at ten years' imprisonment.'

'The case was dropped,' I said.

'We had a hand in that as I expect you realise by now. It could easily be picked up again if we had a change of heart. Our influence with the Customs people is considerable.' He turned back to Sheila. 'Add to that, his motivation. He now knows who killed his cousin and why and that the killer is dying. Case closed, as he might say.'

'Talk anymore about me in the third person,' I said, 'and I'll break your jaw, you smug prick.'

'Talk, talk, talk,' Cummings said. He yawned, stretched his thin arms out, reached under the table, and produced a cut-down automatic shotgun. The strips of duct tape hanging from it made it seem all the more lethal.

Sheila pulled away. 'Seamus, no!'

'It's all right, darlin'. Don't be frightened. I won't hurt any-one if I don't have to. I'll just leave quietly.'

He pointed the gun at Milton-Smith who backed away, his composure disturbed for the first time.

'I'd love to kill you,' Cummings said. 'But what would be the good? There's a million just like you, fuckin' lackeys, manipulators, corrupters. Can't kill 'em all. Don't move, Hardy!'

I'd stood and made a tentative move closer but was still too far from the gun. Casey grabbed at Cummings, but he was drunk and slow and Cummings clubbed him down with the butt of the gun and had it back level all in one smooth movement. Weak as he was, the old skills were still there.

'We'll help you any way we can, Seamus,' Sheila said. 'Won't we, Cliff?'

Cummings laughed, sucked in more breath and said, 'It's all right. I'm thinking I can get to Singapore and contact the *News of the World*.'

'You fool,' Milton-Smith said. 'Put the gun down. We can work something out.'

Cummings slid smoothly towards the door.

'Don't, Seamus,' Sheila said. 'He's got people out there.'

'Bluffing,' Cummings said. 'It was a bonus seeing you again, Sheila.' He opened the door and stepped out.

The single shot had a clean and final sound to it. Cummings was thrown back; he collapsed in the doorway and lay still. A little blood pumped from a wound in his forehead and then stopped.

Sheila burst into tears.

I'd seen the expression of joy on Cummings's face as he'd moved to the door.

'It's all right, love,' I said. 'He knew what he was doing. Don't you see? He set all this up.'

28

The spooks cleaned the decks of course, the way they do. In a very polite operation, the three of us and our cars were removed to what they called their command centre—a house on the outskirts of the Kangaroo Valley township. We waited in a chintzy living room and were served coffee and biscuits.

When he reappeared, Milton-Smith was entirely happy with the outcome and he scarcely bothered to repeat the threats he'd made to Casey, Sheila and me. In a classic piece of spookspeak he thanked Casey and me for leading them to Cummings.

'Cummings was a longstanding piece of unfinished business,' he said. 'Over the years we'd made several attempts to track him down to discover exactly what he knew about our people inside a particular mercenary group.'

'I'm surprised you didn't set Patrick up as a target to flush him out,' I said.

'Not a bad idea, but Malloy was always an unreliable asset.'

'Always?' Sheila said. 'You mean . . .?'

'Oh yes, he was still on the books and was useful from time to time, so we took his assassination quite seriously.'

'I don't buy it,' I said. 'There's been three changes of government in the last twenty years. No one cares now about what dirty tricks you lot got up to back then.'

'I assure you that some very highly placed individuals care very deeply.'

Sheila snorted her disgust. 'What if I say bugger the film and tell the story to the media?'

'You won't.'

'Why not?'

Milton-Smith finished his coffee and put the mug down on a crocheted doily. 'In my office I have a marriage certificate which indicates that Patrick Michael Malloy married one Elizabeth May Jenkins three years before his bigamous union with you. Therefore you are not entitled to inherit his assets.'

'It's probably a forgery,' I said.

'But does Ms Fitzsimmons, no longer in line for a lucrative film role, have the capacity to contest the matter in court?'

Sheila said, 'After talking to you I feel I need a shower.'

On the drive back to Sydney after an edgy night in the motel, Sheila was silent, apart from a few times when she criticised my driving.

The silence and the criticism got to me and I broached what I thought was on her mind.

'You must see that Cummings knew what would happen when he stepped out into the light holding a shotgun. Who wouldn't prefer a quick exit like that to muddling through to the end? Incontinent and doped to the eyeballs with morphine? I would, so would you.'

'Fuck you. How would you know what he was thinking? You don't have a clue what I'm thinking.'

I dropped her at her place in Balmain and she went with scarcely a word. I didn't hear from her for a few days after that and then only to be told that she was going to Melbourne again. She didn't leave a contact number. I phoned and emailed Casey, to see how he was doing and to find out what had happened—what Cummings had told him about the mercenaries and the intelligence service and what Milton-Smith had said about all that and Patrick before Sheila and I arrived. I wanted the full story. I never got a reply. I guessed there wasn't going to be an update of *Diggers for Hire*.

I stopped mourning Patrick; I hadn't really known him.

I got on with the usual things—gym, reading, the pub, Megan and Hank and taking care of my still beating heart. Sheila sent me a text from Melbourne where the film was shooting and I went down to see her but it wasn't a success. She was totally immersed in her role and didn't have any emotion to spare. We quarrelled, and she admitted that she couldn't get the nastiness and the violence she'd been involved in with me out of her head. Couldn't look at me without thinking of Patrick and Cummings and Milton-Smith and lies and blood.

I'll have to wait for the film to come out to see whether it all helped her acting. I expect she'll be good, but, as ever, it'll all depend on the script.